AF350171

Dancing, Dharma
... and Dogs

Dancing, Dharma
... and Dogs

BRIAN PUTNAM

Bywater Press
Bellingham, Washington

Paperback ISBN: 9798218849573.
Library of Congress Catalog Number: 2025923091.
First paperback edition: December 2025.

Cover and interior design by Jeffrey Copeland, Bywater Press, Bellingham, Washington.

Cover image credits:
Moon: Lunar Reconnaissance Orbiter image. Credit: NASA, Goddard Space Flight Center, Arizona State University.
Dogs: Vitalii Arkhypenko via DepositPhotos.
Stars: Son Gallery via Shutterstock.
American Robin: by Rhododendrites – Own work, CC BY, via Wikimedia Commons.
Crow: Péter Gudella via DepositPhotos.

Printed in the USA by Village Books.

2025-12-05

To Robyn, for everything

With special thanks to my brother Dave

PART I : *If it doesn't kill me, will it really make me stronger?*

Pipes. He worked on pipes. His dad was a master plumber, a Leonardo da Vinci when it came to all things sewer and water. Unclogged them, refitted them, replaced them. A plumber by trade. He was short, round, usually jolly, and always surprised at what each day brought. Jeremy's dad was your consummate plumber. A good, old-fashioned, hardworking, butt crack–showing plumber. He worked those pipes, swapped out leaky, over-abused toilets for new, shiny white porcelain models. He liked his work, liked the smiles he brought: the smiles of relief from the gastronomically challenged and those who abhorred even the slightest inkling that human waste existed. Yes, his father's artistry brought relief to many souls whose lives were otherwise often boring and kind of sad. Such is the way of humans.

Jeremy's father loved his job, was proud of the noble profession he'd chosen. He scoffed at those who thought plumbers were lesser than them due to the fact that they worked, at times, with human excrement and slime. He was content and happy with his life, even though he worked long hours and was often called away on weekends. "Money from heaven" he called those gigs. "Most folks think plumbing is a disgusting profession until the toilet is leaking toxic bile and the kids are whining that there is no place to poop. Then a plumber's time is miraculously worth $250 an hour."

Jeremy loved his father. He was genuine, kind, hardworking, and paid attention to him. Jeremy would be waiting for his dad when he pulled the van into the driveway in the evening, smelling of sweat and all those things related to water and sewage, yet also smiling. Out of his van the old man would tumble, a crooked smile on his face, always having time for his boy. Jeremy would run into his big, powerful outstretched arms and the old man would swing him onto his back with one arm and rub his head with the other and ask, "How is my little man?" It brought Jeremy warm peace and comfort.

Jeremy had never met his mother and really didn't know too much about her. She was seldom talked about, and when she was it was usually from a slip by his "uncle," Dwayne, quickly passed over and the subject changed. Jeremy's dad never spoke of her and when he was in the vicinity when a slip occurred, he went silent and his body tensed. Jeremy knew it was not a subject to broach with his dad.

Once, when Jeremy was little and Dwayne was putting him to bed, he asked Dwayne what she was like. His uncle's face flickered in fear for a moment, he looked around to make sure that dad wasn't around, and he put his small round face close to Jeremy's:

"My dear lad," — He had always called Jeremy "lad," and Jeremy had no idea why, and when anyone else attempted that moniker it came out sounding stupid — "your mother was a sweet, quiet woman. Your dear Pa" — that's what Dwayne called him when speaking privately with Jeremy — "loved her very much, and we know she loved you more than the moon and the stars. But she is gone, and speaking of her around your Pa tears him up inside. If it doesn't hurt too much, don't ask. Know that no child is loved more than you are by your dad, me, and, frankly, the universe. I hope that can be enough."

So that was that. Jeremy had listened carefully and silently and nodded solemnly that he understood.

So he watched and listened, which is what he did best. The two men never spoke of her, so him not speaking of her as well seemed to be best.

Dwayne had always been a fixture in Jeremy's life ever since he could remember. Short and balding, Dwayne was a timid, quiet man with a big heart and an uncanny ability to embarrass himself around other people with ease and élan, without ever trying. Hence, he didn't go out much. It wasn't that he tried to make a scene or be an ass — it just seemed as though he could never make the words coming out of his mouth match the thoughts in his head and feelings in his heart.

Among his many talents, Dwayne could cook — boy, could he cook. Not meat and potatoes, not haute cuisine, but deliciousness from the earth. The food was wholesome and natural. Absolutely no meat was cooked in the house except that which lived under water. (Jeremy had never tasted the flesh from a creature that lived above ground; he had never had a burger, and the idea of consuming a cow made him nauseous.) Dwayne created delectability, food for the gods, and lots of it. That food and the beer that was made in the basement created two very large adults in the house. So it was odd that, eat as he did, Jeremy was skinny as a rail.

Jeremy knew very little else about Uncle Dwayne. Didn't even know if he was his real uncle. Jeremy knew this though: Dwayne was kind, loved him dearly, and spent his days trying to make the three inhabitants of the house happy. He lived in the attic, and Jeremy and his dad seldom went up there. Sometimes Jeremy could hear him puttering around upstairs, but that was Uncle D's space, and that was enough for Jeremy to respect it.

Which leads us to Jeremy, the third member of the household, ten years old as this story begins. Easy to frighten and prone to worry, Jeremy was an observer. Named Jeremy Garret Stanislaus, for what it's worth, he preferred listening to talking. He found at an early age that not saying much also made it easier to fade in with the scenery, which he preferred. At this time in his life, if he had been asked to be in a play at school, he would have volunteered to be a rock. A grey, bland one at that. He carefully watched others, listened intently to their conversations or what they might tell him. He seldom spoke; words seemed to never work at capturing what he felt. And feel things he did. He became aware at an early age he was different from others — not in a bad way, and not necessarily good, it just was. He watched when something happened that bothered him. To others it might have seemed to be nothing, but for Jeremy it lingered and always made an impression. Once, in the winter, he watched a poor hummingbird that had stayed for winter struggle to feed itself at their feeder. It struggled to get enough nourishment, struggled to keep at the feeder through the wind and the rain, only to appear lifeless one morning on the back porch. Jeremy contemplated it for what seemed like hours, literally feeling its suffering, until Dwayne and dad came along, shaking their heads and sympathizing with the poor creature's lot in life. They held a funeral for the little thing, buried it, and moved on. For Jeremy, the pain lingered inside of him, and for weeks he would see the feisty creature in his dreams, struggling to survive.

Jeremy watched the world swirl around him and listened quietly, the small skinny boy often feeling invisible and helpless in his feelings.

And that was the household: his old man, sometimes seeming bigger than life; Dwayne, fussing and keeping the family together; and Jeremy, watching, listening, and worrying over the two wonderful humans who took care of him. There they were, a tidy little family tucked away at the end of a dead-end street, surrounded by firs, oaks, and maple trees. The trees created comfort and solitude in an otherwise crowded world, and their mystical wisdom shielded the trio at times from some of the mundane reality that plagues so many. The house was a simple, blue affair, aging gracefully in the Pacific Northwest, enjoying the seasons: the rains of autumn, neatly sandwiched between the beauty of a crisp and sunny day; the blustery cold of January; and the warming air that crept into play as spring gave way to summer. Nestled contently among the trees, the trio was safely ensconced, so it seemed, from some of the cruelty of the world. A pitched roof fit the house, holding an attic at the top and a spacious and spooky basement below. Solemnly looking out at the Cascade mountains, trees standing guard like a protective old dog, made the house their "fortress of solitude."

A robin, perched in the oak trees, watched its nest in the spring, silent and gently tending to all that was below. It appeared to watch over the little outpost of oddity at the end of the street as well, seemingly taking interest in the three creatures who came and left the blue house daily. It was hard to tell how long the robin had lived there, seemingly born to care for this little bit of earth carved out of the planet.

While Jeremy's dad was content with his lot and Jeremy couldn't imagine another life, Uncle D had other ideas. Not that he didn't love his life, it was obvious that he did, but you could see his restlessness, something inside him that was searching for more; yet, his face also told a story of confusion, as though he didn't know what that "more" might be. He always told Jeremy stories — stories of all that he could do and be; for, according to Dwayne, Jeremy could do and be anything he wanted. Anything.

"Explore the world," he would say. "Take some chances, try different things, and visit faraway places. Maybe you could live in a castle and change the world with your creations."

"Someday," D once said, "someday you could work in a big, tall building in the middle of a big, big, ginormous CITY. This palace of opportunity will be so special it will take your breath away."

Jeremy listened politely, or at least tried to. But inside he thought it terrifying. Who in the world would want to spend their days working in a building, never touching the ground?

And then Jeremy would think of his old man, who had his feet firmly on the ground.

Feet on the ground. Jeremy's old man had his feet firmly on the ground, as low and basic as it was. Big, round belly hanging over his belt, and a large, oval, ruddy face. Thick short hands. Strong hands. Calloused and cracked with stubby fingers, but they could make magic. Magic in a faulty pipe, a poop-clogged toilet, or a little boy's dreams. Yeah, sure, they could fix your drain, replace that stinking toilet, make the flood in the basement disappear, or, better yet, make a space shuttle out of cardboard and roller skates. A magician of the drains, flows, and faucets, he was a master plumber and wizard of the imagination, and Jeremy loved him for it. His dad's virtuosity wasn't just in plumbing, though...

Yes, it was the magic the old man created at home in the basement that was truly special. His ability to deftly jury-rig almost anything made him awe-inspiring. Jeremy's dad's artistry at home sometimes lacked perfect technical execution — that wasn't his strong suit, as you shall see — but it was the magic in his creative ideas, in creating a spectacular event out of the most mundane things that made his dad Godlike in Jeremy's mind.

This brings us to a small red bike, made for the smallest of kids, and a bit beat up, at that.

"We don't need a new one. We are gonna make this a fiery chariot of speed and wonder," Dad said one evening after dinner as he finished his second bowl of ice cream. "And you don't need a new one since, while you're learning to ride, you'll be falling all the time and smashing it up at first. And you'll grow out of it in no time. If you survive," he joked.

Jeremy listened politely, a spasm of fear beginning quietly in his stomach and then igniting into a full-fledged typhoon of panic upon hearing the statement "If you survive," which the little boy quickly tried to squash so he could continue to listen politely and focus on a fun-sounding idea: he was going to be riding a bike. Yes, at ten years of age, Jeremy had never been on a bike.

His dad worked his magic during the evenings of that early spring, mists of WD-40 floating in the basement's stale air, wrenches clacking, chains raging, the place smelling of dirt and grease and Dad. Over the evenings that transpired and the bike began to take shape, the excitement welled up inside Jeremy, gathering steam, and became a roiling internal tsunami that grew and grew, pushing Jeremy's insides to the edges, and finally exploding in terror — terror giving way to giddy excitement. Jeremy watched carefully, politely trying to hide his excitement, awe, and wonder. These feelings gathered up like clouds out at sea and began to battle with each other, excitement trying to hang on, but finally making landfall as a full blown storm of terror.

He was going to ride a bike.

He was going to die.

Saturdays passed as the storm raged inside him. Sleep gave way to staring at the ceiling. School work was left like an abandoned, roofless house. And eating? Who could eat with your impending doom, or even splendor, lurking in the basement? Just when Jeremy thought the chariot was complete, his father would step back and examine his work. He would carefully scan the bike, eyeing it as though he was an artist working on his magnum opus. Sometimes he would smile, nod approvingly to himself, and mumble something like, "Nice work, eh? Didn't think you still had it. Good work."

But most often the smile would turn into a slight frown, and occasionally a downright scowl, at which point he would exclaim, "Dag nabbit, we can't have that." And out would come a wrench, or a screwdriver, or perhaps even more of the WD-40, the magic elixir, and he would dive back in — re-truing a wheel, fiddling with the chain, taking off the handlebars and adjusting them a tad, then replacing them. Most of the time, as hard as Jeremy tried, he could not discern any noticeable change. But he watched attentively, nodded his head in agreement with whatever his father decided needed working on in the moment. This bought time for Jeremy, because he knew that someday soon the inevitable would happen, and he would have to mount that steed and try to tame it.

And then, one Saturday morning, it was finished. Jeremy didn't see the bike at first, but he could feel it. The house felt different. He awoke to the smell of coffee, which wasn't unusual. It was everything else that was unusual.

Muffins — he could smell muffins baking. Sweet, moist, raisiny muffins. And bananas. Bananas were only baked in maple syrup for special occasions in Jeremy's household, and then mixed in with strawberries and blueberries for a fruit salad. Muffins and baked bananas. Jeremy's favorite. He slowly rolled over in bed, holding the blanket close to his face. Something was up indeed.

Yes, Jeremy could smell coffee brewing, muffins and bananas baking. He could feel the excitement in the house like it was Christmas or his birthday. These events were not celebrated with fancy gifts and parties, but with revelry and silliness that only his dad could create. And these events were such that they always left you with a little bit of apprehension. That is what the house felt like on that Saturday morning. Something was up. Actually, it was such an auspicious moment Uncle Dwayne and his dad were up together, working on breakfast. He could tell. He could hear them, laughing and music playing. All of this in and of itself was not entirely unplausible, but his dad was seldom up before Uncle D and Jeremy on Saturday, so with everything combined, something big was on the horizon.

And the music was not just regular music — it was *jammin' music*. The laughter only came at the end of the song. They were singing a song. Not just listening to music, but they were singing... kind of... Jeremy could hear it through the heating vent. It was a song of some kind on the stereo, some rock and roll with a big back beat, but over that came two big, rumbling bassos that drowned out everything else.

Sha boom, chaka chaka.

Sha boom chaka, chaka.

Sha boom chaka chaka... **WHUMP!**

Then the sound of laughter, then the song repeated.

This would not end well.

Jeremy slowly began crawling out of bed. Then he heard their next song.

We got to bake zee muffins,

Zee muffins we gots to bake.

Add some tasty carrots,

Some raisins and a snake! **Tee-hee.**

Zen we slice bananas.

And bake them like a cake.

Mix them with some berries,

Slather them in sludge.

Let me eat them all day

Until I cannot budge!

Sha boom, chaka, chaka.

Sha *boom chaka, chaka.* **WHUMP!**

This time **CRASH** as they fell to the floor.

Then laughter. It meant the two were now on the floor, rolling around. You see, the **WHUMP** came from a giant belly collision, and this last time had been so severe, it sent them both sprawling to the floor, hence the **CRASH**. It must have been a major collision, because usually this move, when done with intensity, sent Uncle D across the room and then to the floor. He was that much smaller than Jeremy's dad. This dance had happened a couple of times before, but it was usually late at night while watching some movie. And Uncle D was usually a bit more subdued . . .

Jeremy began his descent down the stairs as the laughter in the kitchen reached a diabolical level. Yes, this was very unusual. He carefully made his way down toward the landing, maneuvering each step of the stairs as if it might be his last, with some type of calamity erupting if he made the wrong move, blowing himself to smithereens by tripping some secret wire lurking on one of the treads. Unsurprisingly, nothing consequential happened. On he went.

But here it was Saturday morning, coffee had been brewed, muffins and bananas baked, and his dad and Uncle D were laughing so hard on the floor that one or both of them would surely pee their pants.

When Jeremy finally made it to the landing, the kitchen came into view and he could see it all. His dad was in his sweats and T-shirt, which meant he had been up all night or gotten up in a hurry very early in the morning.

The two men were still sprawled on the floor, giggling, when Jeremy surveyed the room, at first unnoticed. He looked at them with a mix of fondness and worry — worry for them, but mostly for himself.

He now knew what was coming. The bike, it had to be the bike. There they were, his two stalwart caretakers, giggling uncontrollably as they wiggled on the floor.

Excitement was in the air.

An olfactory extravaganza met Jeremy as he came off the stairway, beginning with his nose then enveloping his entire being. He knew what was up, and knew he should be worried, but all the delicious smells and the two crazy men lying on the floor made the anxiety take a back seat to the hunger and excitement that was building in him as he stared at the breakfast laid out on the table. Like a condemned man heading to his last meal, he threw caution to the wind and focused on the meal.

The three sat after breakfast, looking off into space. Jeremy, for all his anxiety, could not resist a breakfast like this, and even though he tried to be tender as he ate, his tastebuds overtook him and he swallowed down three muffins and two bowls of fruit, homemade kefir, and nuts. Oh, and a bit of maple syrup. Yum.

The old man sat back, licking his lips, patting his belly.

"Aren't you going to guess?" his dad asked, giving Jeremy a wink and a smile.

Jeremy shook his head.

"Not even a little guess?"

Headshake. Jeremy knew.

"It's finished."

What, the crucifixion?

"Well?"

"Well?" Dwayne chimed in.

Jeremy looked on.

"I do believe it is time to try this puppy out."

His dad, of course, was not referring to a canine. It was the bike.

Jeremy sat staring. He absolutely did not know what to say. He knew he had some kind of crooked grin on his face, desperately trying to keep it plastered there so it didn't give way to the wide-eyed, open-mouthed look of trepidation that was hiding under his cheeks. It was kind of like opening a Christmas present you save until last because you were sure it was something cool, but it turns out to be a sweater. You certainly don't want to disappoint the anxious faces staring at you, but it isn't really what you wanted at all. Jeremy smiled and tried to nod in excitement. It suddenly occurred to him that it might just appear he was spastically bobbing his head as though having some type of seizure. He wasn't sure. However, he felt he had conveyed some sort of agreement with the two men — that he was ready to "try this puppy out" as it were, to ride that bike like a champ — for after an awkward moment of silly looks being exchanged, Dwayne nervously reached his hand out and shook Jeremy's knee. The old man chortled, grunted from the full belly weighing him down, and started the procession to the living room.

The three solemnly walked, in single file, to the living room window. And there it stood.

The bike.

There it was in the driveway, now very real. Larger than life. Sure, he had watched his old man work on it over the previous five Saturdays in the basement, but now it was real. Jeremy had somehow not made the connection firmly in his young brain that the completion of the bike's resurrection would in fact lead to him riding the thing.

But there it stood, this red stallion of Satan, surely a prototype for one of the four horsemen of the apocalypse, ready to take him to oblivion. Before it had seemed to be a small, rusted, insignificant low-speed training bike, but now it had reincarnated. Yes, the front tire had been transformed into a giant bull's head, or maybe it was that of a Minotaur? Perhaps Beelzebub's raging bull of universal destruction, with smoke now coming from its flared nostrils, the handlebars now horns — poisonous lances of destruction. And that beautiful banana seat his father and Dwayne had purchased as a surprise to spruce the thing up? A cobra waited in its stead to bite his butt and send Jeremy, writhing and screaming, straight into the grasp of the devil himself.

Jeremy shook his head. It was a bike, for criminy's sake; a little red bike, spruced up by his dad, and he was going to ruin the day by overreacting and terrifying himself. It was a little red bike, and he would love riding the thing!

His dad was beaming, proud of his handiwork, his ample stomach gurgling with delight from the scrumptious breakfast from which the coffee had jolted him alive. Jeremy vowed to enjoy this moment, telling himself he would soon be whizzing around the neighborhood, waving to the folks down the street — neglecting, of course, the fact that he never spoke to the neighbors let alone looked or waved at them. No, this was going to be a splendid, triumphant day.

Looking at Uncle D off to the side diminished that promise, as his dear uncle was gently wringing his hands and chewing his lower lip, all the while attempting a courageous smile.

Stay the course, Jeremy thought. A good day this will be.

His dad strode down to the driveway, slipped the bike through an arm and slung it over his shoulder.

"Showtime."

The old doofus giggled as he walked, a little hitch in his step as he walked toward the street.

Jeremy followed.

He was going to ride a bike, and he was most certainly NOT going to die.

Jeremy didn't die, of course. The two lumbered down the driveway while Dwayne stood uneasily on the porch. Jeremy and his dad made their way to the street, the old man in the lead with the bike hanging from him like a little toy. The old man could just have easily been a Roman centurion taking the burden of the cross from Christ, with Jeremy, bearing the weight of humankind's sins on his soul, going to meet God.

Jeremy loved that man ever so much and, not wanting to be disrespectful or rude, he carefully listened to the instructions given and clambered over the bike and got it between his legs.

"I got you, little man," said his dad, steadying the bike by holding the seat, which reassured Jeremy. His big hands held the handlebars as well. The bike felt good beneath him, and he trusted his dad, with the view of his big body and the smell of sweat, coffee, and breakfast reassuring him. This was going to work out — God forbid, it might be fun!

"You jest put your hands there, feet on the pedals. I'm here with you, to steady you. We'll be fine. This contraption is going to set you free; it will open the world to you, Jer. You will be able to roam the planet at will."

His dad was truly excited and happy for Jeremy and was sure that it was just a little bit of anxiety in the boy, a few butterflies that would fly away when the wind was blowing in his face. It never crossed his mind that the little boy might be scared stiff.

And they began. Jeremy and his dad started down the street together at a very slow pace, his dad's hands on the bike as he walked beside him, a big smile on his face. As they progressed, he broke into a slow trot. Jeremy felt good: he felt strong and proud of himself. He would not let fear get the best of him. It was exhilarating. The old man was beside him, whispering to Jeremy words of pride and reassurance as his breath slowly became more and more labored as they picked up speed.

With every turn of the pedal, Jeremy became less fearful and more excited, soon bordering on the ecstatic. He was riding a bike?! No death in sight...

The wind was in his face. Jeremy was grinning now, beginning to pedal faster and faster. The grumpy lady down the street, Mrs. King, stood motionless, staring as Jeremy whizzed by. How could she stay standing on those old, wobbly legs as the slipstream from his Mach speed passing by must have blasted her — like getting too close to a rocket? A strange man in a weird hat, walking his dog, gave him a little wave and a warm yet crooked smile. Time stopped at that moment. The universe itself took a break to appreciate the event. Jeremy was strong and confident and in control now. With him and his dad taking on the world, a bit of his fear and trepidation waned for a moment. Jeremy could hear and sense his old man was struggling beside him; his grip was not quite as firm, and he could sense his old man's breath becoming more labored. But Jeremy was lost in the experience; it was sublime . . .

"You're doing it, little man. You go Jer!"

And, suddenly, Jeremy realized he was alone on the bike. He was pedaling on his own, terror and ecstasy battling for control of his mind as he hoped he could stop the motion but not wanting to at the same time. His face flashed from a giant grin to a grimace of terror — back and forth, back and forth, as he frantically pedaled. Flying down the street, Jeremy made a quick glance over his shoulder — in retrospect ill-advised — to see his dad back in the distance, his face almost blue and his arm upraised, dancing what appeared to be some kind of spastic jig, becoming more bloated and winded at each moment, cackling like a giant leprechaun stomping the pavement and shouting encouragement. Behind that, Uncle Dwayne stood out in the street, wringing his hands and bouncing with excitement.

"You go, lad!" Uncle D cried. "Don't look back!"

Jeremy took his uncle's advice and turned forward to focus on the road ahead. He was streaming down the street most assuredly, wind wailing in his ears, the bike lapping up the asphalt like a thirsty horse, and he could swear he heard the neighborhood cheering him on.

Jeremy soon realized he was slowly, incrementally but quite indubitably, heading for the right side of the street. Maneuvering the bike had never crossed his mind, but it seemed as though now might be a good time to seriously consider the endeavor.

"Steer!" he could hear his father scream in the distance. "Put the damn brakes on!"

Brakes, now there was a thought.

Almost instantaneously, the fear that had turned to exhilaration made a major directional shift, gearing up into fear overdrive, and in his psyche a frantic terror attempted to overthrow his entire being, throwing his emotions into the gear of exquisite freaked-outness. The cogs inside were wrenching and tearing at him, and Jeremy valiantly stood up to fight it a bit, just a bit…

But steer? He didn't know how and, quite frankly, his arms and legs and torso had fallen into a kind of rigor mortis. And brake? What was this term, brake, that the possessed leprechaun being behind him that once was his old man was screaming about?

"For criminy's sake, stop the bike, Jeremy!" He could hear his father shouting from what seemed an interminable distance.

Jeremy couldn't hear or see Uncle D, but knew he must be more anxious than his father was.

Brakes? Somewhere in a corner of his mind, Jeremy remembered his dad had mentioned pushing back on the pedals to stop. Huh? How?

It quickly became quite clear that if Jeremy didn't stop or steer soon, he would be engaging intimately with the rear bumper of Mr. Fitzpatrick's prized and restored '64 baby blue Plymouth Valiant. You know the kind: push-button transmission, bucket seats — a working man's Ferrari. It came quickly to his mind that there would be a great deal of physical pain associated with the interaction, pain Jeremy wanted to avoid at all costs, as smashing into the back of a parked car was not yet on the bucket list. And it also flashed in his mind the yearslong anguish he would endure for harming that penultimate Plymouth. They would surely need to move out of the neighborhood in shame. For a few moments Jeremy had seen himself as the dashing darling of the street, but if he became the kid who killed Mr. Fitzpatrick by breaking his old heart, he would carry shame.

Mind you, all the above thoughts occurred in the span of a few seconds, if that, before he pushed down hard on one of the pedals. This, of course, did not work to stop him because the family had long forgotten that this was a "training bike" as they said in the '60s and didn't have any stinking brakes. His foot fell off the pedal, causing his crotch to smash into the brand new banana seat, further causing him to stand up straight in agony, which allowed him to watch clearly, in slow motion and living color, as he smashed into the back of the valiant Valiant. In the distance he could hear his old man and Uncle Dwayne exclaiming, "Holy smoking rockets," and "oh dear, oh dear."

Jeremy stayed suspended on the stalled bike for a moment and then tumbled off, landing as a crumpled heap in the street. The little red bike stayed upright for a second more, as if making its last stand, and then fell unceremoniously onto the little boy. Motionless on the ground, Jeremy wondered what injuries he had sustained and how he could even be breathing after the crash of the century. Since he and the bike had been travelling at a real-time speed of slightly over three miles per hour, the injuries to Jeremy, not counting his pride, were few, if any. However, since Jeremy thought he must have been flying at least at thirty gazillion miles per hour, he was sure he had broken at least twenty bones.

In retrospect, it might have been better if Jeremy lost consciousness, but he didn't. He was in a stupor of fear and humiliation. He lay on the street, not sure what to do. He could hear the frightened comments of adults speaking above him but could only make out bits and pieces of what they were saying. What he was able to gather was that the grownups had pronounced him not dead and in no need of an ambulance. His father gently picked him up. He could tell it was his dad for a few reasons, like the caring arms that held him, but mostly from his smell. The smell of his father always calmed him down, strange as it might seem. Those two things brought him some solace, so he decided it might be best to just melt into the old man and hope the rest of the world disappeared. He curled physically and figuratively into himself. Jeremy retreated into a kind of suspended animation and waited until he felt the calm and comfort that was all around begin to ease the fear within him. When he finally did get his wits about himself, he observed he was up in Uncle Dwayne's attic room under a blanket on the couch, a cup of chamomile tea on a little table beside him.

The first things Jeremy noticed after coming back to his senses were the warm quilt around him and the pillow propping him up on the couch. Then he smelled the tea — sweet chamomile tea with a mixture of things he could not discern, nor did he try, but he knew all of this meant Uncle Dwayne was close by, working his paternal magic. As he slowly opened his eyes and they began to focus, he confirmed he was indeed on Uncle D's couch. A high ceiling hovered above, a large window was to his left, and Uncle Dwayne sat at the end of the couch with Jeremy's feet in his lap. His uncle wore a worried, caring face as he looked at Jeremy, willing the boy to be better. Uncle D's expression slightly brightened as Jeremy opened his eyes.

"You did well today, lad."

Well? He had done well?!?!

Yeah, right, he did a good job of crashing the beauty of a bike his dad had fixed up for him. Surely he had wreaked havoc on the beautiful Valiant of Mr. Fitzgerald, no doubt causing thousands of dollars of damage or, worse yet, totaling the car completely.

"Yes, my lad, you were very brave. Brave in the fact that you didn't do it for yourself, but for your dad and me, and did not let fear get the best of you. And you tried with all your might. You conquered that fear for a bit, and you felt that wonderful feeling when you did, didn't you, eh?"

The boy's eyes grew wide.

"Then the fear got ahold of you again, as it often does. But no matter; this will make you stronger, and those inner demons in you will one day vanish."

Jeremy stared in silence.

"And remember my boy, you are still small, the bike is fine, and Mr. Fitzpatrick's old car got away with barely a scratch. It will give him something to work on and give him plenty of stories to tell over coffee with his cronies. I'll make him a crock of goulash, that will settle him. You rest here a bit. Let your thoughts settle, steady your breathing, and let your mind clear. A clear, quiet mind might be just what you need. It might bring about a comfort in you that you never realized was there."

Dwayne stood, set Jeremy's feet on the couch, and silently descended the stairs, leaving the scared and tired little boy with his thoughts. And there he sat, the blanket wrapped around him like he was a druid, cup of tea in his hands, clutching it as though he was Jeremy at ninety, old and feeling tired and done. The cup warmed his hands, allowing a release to radiate up his arms and through his body, relaxing him a bit. He took a sip of the tea, letting it course through his veins with tenderness.

Dwayne's words played over and over, creating a strange tune that circled around his young mind. He'd done well?

According to Dwayne, he had. His uncle's words swam around the brain, his dad's laugh coming into the scene, thoughts of the trepidation that had slowed his descent down to breakfast, all intermingled into a confusing, cerebral mush of polenta. His fear had made it so he was almost unable to get on the bike. Then the feeling of freedom and being alive finally overtook him and filled him with confidence and exhilaration, squashing the fear without him even knowing it and, with that release, everything had become more real. He swore now that, in retrospect, he could see the individual rhinestones on the black glasses Mrs. King wore, eyebrows arched over them as Jeremy whizzed by on his mount. Wasn't there a distinct scent of lavender in the air at the very moment he passed her? Jeremy was sure of it. And the stranger with the dog? Had he come purposely to watch Jeremy and urge him on?

Yes, there might be a hint of truth in the words Uncle D had uttered. As he sat sipping his tea, Jeremy realized that at some point during his reverie a robin had situated herself on the windowsill of the large attic window and appeared to be watching him, carefully assessing his state of being. He assessed the bird back. He was sure it was the same robin he had seen before around the front yard of the house. He closed his eyes for a moment, as it was impossible the bird was really watching *him*.

Jeremy brought his attention back to the attic, hoping the bird would eventually fly off searching for a nice worm to munch. The attic was a simple affair, typical of a 1920s bungalow that is ubiquitous in America. Unpainted wood with exposed beams formed the ceiling, arching up to a cityscape of cobwebs and dust, a large window facing out toward the street and a Douglas fir that always kept watch over the house. Dwayne's domain was quite tidy, with a couch facing the window, a counter with a sink, and a hot plate, plates, cups, and silverware laid out neatly. By the teapot on the counter were also assorted jars with what appeared to be herbs and spices in them, along with an old-fashioned scale, a mortar and pestle, and, on the wall above them, a tapestry that Jeremy did not understand. The moon and planets were there, along with words in some language he had never seen. The one time Jeremy had asked Dwayne about all these things, Jeremy was simply told not to worry about them and never, ever touch the jars. That was enough for Jeremy, and he let it be.

Nervously glancing back to the window, Jeremy noticed the bird had not left. There it sat, and now he was sure the beak had cracked a slight smile. The thing was in no hurry to leave, so Jeremy decided to continue the interaction and see what might happen. There they sat for a moment, eye to eye, the robin nonplussed as it contemplated

Jeremy, and Jeremy returned the gaze. There they sat. The bird looked at Jeremy as if she knew what he was thinking, staring at him intently. Time stopped for a bit, though he wasn't sure how long — a minute or an hour? Who knew? The bird and the boy gazed at each other, sharing a moment of compassion and understanding. Jeremy *knew*, he knew the bird knew him deep inside, and there was comfort, astounding comfort, in that.

Jeremy's thoughts stopped. From the far reaches of his mind he could hear a soft voice, but he couldn't understand the words. He breathed deeply and his body relaxed. The words became more audible now, the voice one he had never heard before: a woman's voice. "Welcome the fear, don't push it away, little one. It will all be okay. You have tremendous things to do in this world if you can befriend your fear." The robin suddenly cocked its head, dipped its beak a bit as if to nod in acceptance, and flew off. It had been a curious day.

This may not seem like much, but those few moments in the attic sunk into Jeremy's psyche and would remain with him for the rest of his life, always working behind the scenes.

Still looking in the direction of where the robin had sat, Jeremy's mind drifted outside the window, trying to catch a glimpse of the bird as it flew toward the fir tree. Jeremy mulled over and over the events of the day, beginning with the fear he experienced while walking down the stairway and the joy at eating his favorite foods with his dad and his uncle. Then the crazy way that, in a manner of minutes, the day moved from terror to ecstasy and back to terror again. Uncle D's words firmly imprinted themselves in his mind.

His thoughts were suddenly interrupted by the sound of the two men trying in vain to tiptoe up the stairs. It was kind of like trying to sneak up on someone when you're wearing ski boots while walking on gravel: It didn't work too well.

First one head appeared through the hole in the floor where the stairs emerged, then another. The steps were in the middle of the room, a flimsy, slated arm rail surrounding three sides of the stairs. Two round heads appeared through the slats, just enough so only the eyes appeared above the floor. Jeremy smiled behind the quilt as he watched the two through squinted eyes, pretending to be asleep.

"Is he really okay?" asked his dad.

"He's fine," replied Uncle D.

"You sure?"

"I'm sure."

"Surely sure?" His dad fell apart when Jeremy felt puny. And right now, the old guy needed lots of reassurance.

"Yes, I am completely sure."

"Should we wake him up?"

"No, let him be."

"Okay."

There was silence for a moment.

"Psst, Jeremy. You awake?" His dad just couldn't stand it.

Uncle D rolled his eyes.

Jeremy faked a yawn and stretched his arms. Seeing he was, in fact, awake, the two men scurried up the rest of the stairs and hurried toward Jeremy — just what the little boy wanted. He smiled to himself. Yes, that was exactly what he wanted, to be fussed over for the rest of the day by these two rotund, lovable galoots.

– – –

So that was Jeremy's life as it tumbled along. From the outside, things like this would appear to be kind of exciting — and perhaps it would be fun and exciting if it happened occasionally. But craziness and the unexpected were not uncommon in Jeremy's world, tempered at times by incursions of calming and serene interactions, like the one with the robin and Uncle Dwayne in the attic. Jeremy looked forward to those moments and tried to understand what happened within him so he could learn to recreate them. It was just that, for Jeremy, his mind was so full of thoughts and images. The constant cascade of thoughts crashing into one and other created the fear that his world could explode at any moment.

And, eventually, the explosion occurred. To get to that event we must span eight years. Time went by like a circular circus, one event crashing into the next like dominoes. Schoolwork to attend to and the unknown future loomed over Jeremy like an undulating fog, never allowing him to quite discern exactly the path he should take, and left to wonder if life would offer him to the adult world with his feet on the ground or teetering precariously way up in the sky.

Jeremy went to school. He was quite popular, believe it or not. He learned to push the fear and trepidation of being alive inside and interact with the world as if his fears didn't exist. It became apparent to him that by keeping one's mouth shut, most people thought you were agreeable, affable, and smart. Thank goodness no one was able to look inside at the tempest raging in his head. Jeremy grew like a weed and found friends in high school. He even played Merlin in the school's production of *Camelot*. Acting came easy to Jeremy. He quickly realized that when taking on a part he was just swapping out one mask for the other, which made it entertaining in a strange way. Jeremy Stanislaus's life moved along with him always feeling a bit on the outside, looking in, trying to make the best out of the things life threw his direction. That's when his fears finally became reality.

PART II: *Fall is doing the dance, but Winter plays the tune.*

Queen Anne's lace, or the wild carrot, as it is also named, grows in abundance in the Pacific Northwest of the United States. Not to be confused with its deadly cousin, a version of hemlock, its white-latticed flowers pepper the outside rim of fields, earnestly growing in hopes of becoming a splendiferous harvest. As summer begins to wane, succumbing to the heat and dry air that July, August, and September brought, the beautiful white blossoms begin to fade, dropping their seeds as they begin to die. As the process continues, Queen Anne's lace emits a scent that is at the same time sweet and thick, yet hints of an almost burnt decay. As the days roll by, the scent becomes stronger and more enchanting. The smell of death and decaying plant life makes it seem like the earth is finally giving in to the eons it has spun, suspended by the myth of gravity around the sun. For many who live in the Pacific Northwest the smell is comforting and addictive, portending the crisp, bright fall evenings to come. And with that comes the dying of the lace, ushering autumn out and bringing winter into bloom.

It was this time of year, September through October, that Jeremy loved so much. And it was on one such summer's day before Jeremy headed off to college that he and his dad embarked on an "adventure." This term Jeremy had adopted many years ago for some reason, and it'd stuck. Adventures celebrated a new beginning. Actually, it was a letting go of the old adventures and turning to a new chapter of adventures.

Adventures for these two consisted of climbing into the old pickup and wandering back roads aimlessly, no destination in mind until the destination presented itself and, suddenly, they had arrived. The pair always discovered something new; it might be a country grocery store they had never noticed or perhaps a turn they had never seen that took them to a beautiful piece of water. It was never anything special — or, more accurately, *always something special.*

Driving back from the beach on this late afternoon, they stopped at the Blarney Castle, a decrepit old restaurant and bar with plywood turrets tacked on the roof to resemble a faux castle. For some reason it was painted green and white, perhaps to give it an Irish flair. At least they didn't attempt to paint on faux stone, thank God. There the two stopped: onion rings and soda for Jeremy, a delicacy they never had at his house, and beer for dad. Jeremy always looked forward to these visits and dreaded them at the same time. He loved eating the special treat but it inevitably made him sick to his stomach, and when he got home the treatment was chamomile tea and crackers from Uncle Dwayne. Jeremy and his dad enjoyed sitting in these dark old places, usually finding a table off to the side, his dad joking with the regulars and Jeremy listening intently to the old geezers' stories. Jeremy was by now an expert at nodding when he thought it was appropriate, laughing if others seemed to think it was funny, and always happy to let them rib him for his youth. A perfect day was one during which nobody asked Jeremy a question that required speaking.

As the late summer light was fading, the two wandered back to the truck. It didn't drive very well and rust surrounded the fading yellow paint, but it oozed comfort and familiarity, which was nice. Jeremy's dad sat in the cab and sighed.

"This has been a great day, Jeremy. Thanks," his dad began. "You'll be heading out soon, and this will be our last adventure together; at least one like this. I'm going to miss you. Remember that bike I fixed up for you, the one you crashed?" Jeremy smiled and nodded. "Think about that time. Remember it. You were scared to death, but you got through it." He then turned and stared at Jeremy. "Remember Jer, things are seldom as they seem. Fear has a way of covering reality with layers of lies, twisting and screwing with what you think. Your mom was good at cutting through all that. God, I miss her." Jeremy smiled and tried not to look startled. It was the first time his dad had ever spoken like that. It was a side of him that Jeremy had never seen before, as this kind of talk usually fell on Uncle D.

His dad continued. "Just try to remember that when you are scared and alone. I hate to be the one to tell you, but it's going to happen. And try to remember that there is so much more going on that we small humans don't have a clue about. Finally, and then I'll shut up: the universe embraces the goofiness that life offers up. Promise me you won't forget that." Jeremy stared at his dad. He had never loved the man more. He didn't understand everything he had just heard, but he knew it must be very important.

With that, Jeremy's dad started the truck and slowly headed east, toward home.

The drive back on these trips with the old man were special to Jeremy, as time with him alone and the beach's atmosphere seemed to slow his dad down, and heading home had a quiet, wistful feel to it. Once they descended the coast range into the valley, they took to the back roads slowly and comfortably. The last of the summer wheat had been harvested, and the cooling late September day brought the feel and smell of decayed grass, and the drying, slow demise of the Queen Anne's lace filled the air, making Jeremy sleepy and a bit sad. As they lumbered over the rolling hills, getting ready to crest that last hill before a long, soft decline brought them down to the valley floor and then home, he knew what time it was.

"Think we can do it, Jer?" His dad asked. Times like these are when you savor every second of being alive, because these are the moments in time that matter. These are the times we remember as special. "Do you really think we can?"

Jeremy nodded and smiled for the old man. The coasting record; they were going to try, as they always did, for the record. He couldn't remember when this game started, or why, but his dad got extreme pleasure from it, and that was all that mattered. As they rolled to a stop at the top of the hill, the front wheels kissing the decline, the old man took the truck out of gear and stopped. He looked solemnly at Jeremy, the corners of his mouth giving away his delight.

"Gotta be brave at heart."

Jeremy nodded.

"Gotta be pure of spirit."

Jeremy nodded harder, smiling up at his father.

"And you *gotta* be sincere."

Jeremy vigorously nodded in agreement, a smile breaking around the corners of his mouth.

"Here we go."

Slowly, ever so slowly, the old man lifted his foot off the brake, his overly dramatic solemnity almost breaking as his glee for the whole endeavor tried to take over.

The truck began to roll down the hill. Very slowly at first and then picking up speed as gravity pulled them onward.

The record. Jeremy knew the routine by heart. At the bottom of the small hill the road bottomed out into the valley, straightening out toward the horizon. In the distance, Jeremy had no idea how far, stood an old oak on the side of the road, all alone and somber, committed to watching the valley for eternity, acknowledging the old truck as it picked up speed.

"Here we go, my boy. Gonna make it past the tree tonight. A world record."

This was it. They were going for the record. The "world record," whatever that meant. Jeremy began to uncontrollably grin; he knew what was coming. His father turned the lights off on the truck, and the rust bucket glided into the fading light, making it surreal and awesome. Out of nowhere the dial-up radio in the cab started playing an old country song, sad and slow. Through his excitement, Jeremy felt his old inner fear start to wiggle around deep inside.

The old man scrunched down, looking through the windshield under the rim of the steering wheel. His mirth almost burst from his lips, the joy of the moment enveloping him.

Jeremy scrunched, too. To reduce the wind resistance? Channel their energy to defy gravity and move the truck onward faster to meet their goal? Jeremy had absolutely no idea, but to do otherwise would shatter the moment. Down they went, hitting the bottom of the hill at breakneck speed, or so it seemed to Jeremy, as they flattened out and began their quest toward the tree.

The coasting record.

As the truck moved further they began to uncontrollably bounce in their seats, the truck slowing as they reached the bottom of the hill, but moved forward nonetheless. There, in the dusk, loomed the tree. Jeremy wanted to believe its limbs were arms that would scoop them up in victory if they made it there, but an acorn of fear still remained. Beside the tree was a man — a farmer, Jeremy figured — wearing the weirdest hat he'd ever seen, sitting and watching. A dog sat at his side.

Finally, his dad could not control himself, and he began to giggle and then roar in laughter.

"We're gonna do it, little man, we're gonna do it."

Jeremy was bouncing harder now, grinning like his dad, completely at a loss as to what would happen if they did get to the tree, but knew it was within reach.

"C'mon boy, we can do it!"

They began to rock back and forth, urging the truck forward. Suddenly, his dad rolled the window down, slapping the side of his door. The laughter built as they rocked, as if the father and son were urging gravity to bend to their will, to be a player in this grand event.

"Whooooo weeeeeeee!!! It's gonna happen, we're gonna do it!"

Cackling uncontrollably, the two willed the truck further, inching along now, closer to the tree than Jeremy could ever remember. Finally, it was over. The wheels came to a stop with the bed of the truck just past the tree. Jeremy noticed the man with the hat and the dog were gone.

"My God, boy, we did it. We did it!"

The old man leaned into his son, his boy, laughing like Jeremy had never heard him laugh. Jeremy threw his arms around his dad, just loving the joy, loving the moment.

"We did it! We did it! We d — "

Just like that, the old man slumped into Jeremy, motionless, pinning the boy against the car's door.

PART III: *Pieces of a life sometimes disintegrate.
What replaces it is often very strange, yet beautiful.*

Jeremy is now Stan. His last name was Stanislaus, and after college
when he came to the city and began working in the Big Place, as he
referred to it in his mind, Stan was the name that stuck. He couldn't
clearly recall what events transpired to make the name change happen. He vaguely remembered a supervisor who couldn't remember
his name calling him Stanislaus after glancing at his resume. The
supervisor shortened it to Stan in a meeting and, with that, Jeremy
became Stan. Not wanting to rock the boat or be a squeaky wheel,
Jeremy let it slide and the next thing he knew the world was calling
him Stan. Jeremy hated the name but kept silent and let the feeling
sink to the bottom of his stomach, where it festered. Sitting in a meeting now, he was trying hard to remember how he had ever ended up
in this job. As he searched his mind for an answer, Jeremy began to
try to find a good reason to make such a choice.

You see, things had not gone perfectly since his dad's demise.
The years that followed were all kind of a blur. Once the shock, terror,
and disbelief had subsided regarding the terrifying day in the truck,
he and Dwayne began pretending at life again. Time went by at an
uneventful, Jell-O-like pace. They went through the motions of being
a family, partaking in meals and the usual activities that went on in
the house.

When the old man abruptly left the planet, Jeremy was in his last
summer at home before college. With his dad's death, that new page

in his life was postponed until the following year, as Jeremy needed more time to put his life back in order — or, at least, attempt to gather himself. The days flew by, but nothing happened; it was like a dense fog had descended upon the house. The days took on a twilight zone quality, with nothing feeling particularly pleasant or real.

Dwayne's sparkle became dulled. He still smiled, offered sage advice, and was warm, kind, and loving. Yet he was different. He began to take the truck on "walkabouts," little trips for a few days so he could have some solitude and "collect" his thoughts, as he would say. Jeremy wasn't so sure. Uncle D always returned looking tired and a bit distant, without many tales to share about his excursions.

On one of Dwayne's trips, Jeremy sat alone in the old house feeling vacant. He felt very alone. Lonely alone. And very sad. It seemed everyone who meant something to him had just disappeared without much warning. His old man, and Dwayne for all intents and purposes, it seemed, had abandoned him. Jeremy had an image in his mind of a robin on a windowsill; had it been a memory or merely his imagination? He could clearly see the robin's eyes, looking knowingly and gently at him. Where had he seen it before? Somewhere in the recesses of his brain he remembered that robin. A robin trying to convey something. Then the memory, like the bird, was gone.

After sitting for who-knows-how-long by himself in the house one day, he wandered down to the basement, thinking maybe he should just pull up a chair and dig into the vats of home brew that lived down there. The bottles had sat untouched since his dad died. Jeremy sat there for hours, a beer on the card table going warm and stale. It just didn't seem like the answer. Then, without really thinking, Jeremy got up and wandered toward the attic, to Dwayne's room.

He hadn't been there in at least a couple of years. An old quilt, looking awfully familiar, sat on the couch, and Jeremy knew he needed to wrap that thing around him and hunker down. And hunker he did.

The light of the day faded to darkness, and somewhere down the line he drifted off to sleep. He woke up as the horizon could be seen through the window, bringing morning to the world. He watched this cycle for one, two, three more times, he wasn't sure, his brain empty but aching. Then, one dark evening, he felt a hand on his shoulder. Jeremy slowly turned and there was Dwayne, looking kindly down at him.

"Lad. I am so sorry. I shouldn't have left you like that. I raced back as soon as I heard."

Heard what?

"I know better, and I shouldn't have needed to be told."

Told what? By whom?

It was as if Dwayne knew Jeremy's thoughts. "I hope that some-day you will meet them. But never mind, dear boy. You have much bigger issues to deal with right now. Your grief is immense. As well it should be."

Jeremy must have looked strangely at his uncle. Dwayne re-turned the stare with kindness and compassion.

"It will all work out; someday you will see. We will get through this together."

Jeremy would never forget the rest of the rest of their time together until college began.

Dwayne and Jeremy spent time together just sitting, walking, cooking, and fiddling in the garden. Sometimes they would sit and chat about the old man, but most of the time it wasn't necessary. The old man was always there with them; they could both feel his presence. Bringing him up felt kind of like talking about someone who is in the room and, for some reason, you don't think they can hear what you are saying. The time was quiet and peaceful; melancholy, but nice. Try as he might, Dwayne could not shake Jeremy from his pain. As for Jeremy, he really believed he was trying to come out of his melancholy, to put his father's death in perspective and move on, but he just couldn't. Once again, deep down in his stomach, a flicker of fear began to grow. Even after a wonderful day with his uncle, Jeremy would lie down in bed only to feel the embers of his fear begin again. What in the world was to become of him? Why did he feel so alone? The questions would spin in his mind for hours until he would drift into a dreamless, fitful sleep.

And then Jeremy was out of the house, off to school. Off to make do on his own. The college years were not particularly memorable for Jeremy. The time he spent at school gave way to more and more fear of the future. Worries about what to do with himself and a sense that at any time another horrible thing would happen kept Jeremy constantly on edge. His fears of things he had no control over kept building and weighing him down inside, creating a kind of angst he had never felt before and couldn't find any way to stop. The fear and pain built up and pushed him to such a state of trepidation that he immersed himself in studying to be something, anything. Jeremy dove into the world of computer codes and algorithms, facts and data, nothing that really made sense deep down, but somehow would save him from his fear.

He did very well in in the academic world, or so it seemed, as he was praised by those in positions of authority and, on paper, he looked to be a genius. As his time at school began to wind down, his peers and acquaintances, as he had no real friends to speak of, looked on in envy at the opportunities that awaited him. However, none of this could shake the fear that had taken up permanent residence in the pit of his stomach.

As for his relationship with Dwayne, it turned out that they spent less and less of Jeremy's vacations together. His uncle was preoccupied most of the time, plus Jeremy felt awkward at the house. Eventually the trips home gave way to taking summer classes or internships and the like, so when he moved to a tiny apartment and took a job after school, he did so on his own. Jeremy and Dwayne eventually stopped communicating altogether. The fear inside made it so Jeremy no longer trusted anyone, even Dwayne. For Jeremy, trusting other humans only led to very bad things happening. It was easier on one's own.

_ _ _

And now here he was: Stan, of all names, doing not-sure-what, sitting in yet another meeting. He had really had enough, but he had no idea how to remedy the situation. The conference room where Stan, née Jeremy, sat was a bland, windowless box. There were three walls he could see, his back against the door. On one wall was a whiteboard, on another a projector screen, and the third wall contained two "inspirational" posters. One poster contained a picture of a seagull flying. Under it was a statement that ended with the word "soar" in large letters. On the other was a picture of a ladder with a word on each step. The final step held the word "success." Stan had no clue as to what messages they were trying to convey. The one with the bird made him want to go to the beach. With his workload as it was right now, that wasn't going to happen anytime soon. The second one, of the ladder, was downright creepy. Stan was terrified of falling off ladders. Who could be successful standing on the top step? Everyone in the civilized world knew you weren't supposed to stand on the top step of a ladder. There were big warning signs pasted right on them.

Yes, he had had enough. There was no point to this. His fear had not abated, only grown more and more intense, his work more and more meaningless. There had to be something else about this business of living. His brain was through. He was no Stan. He was Jeremy. Enough nonsense. But, once again, no solution presented itself. At the moment, he was just trying to be invisible. On the screen in front of him was the project image of a graph of some kind, but Jeremy hadn't been listening so he had no idea what it referred to. Lost in his own world of terror, Jeremy had assumed his deep-in-thought pose. His hands were clasped and his chin rested on them, his eyes closed, and his head slightly bent. This was his go-to position for when he didn't want to talk or have any questions tossed his way. His team members assumed he was listening deeply and knew not to bother him. Some incredible idea must be percolating in his mind, they erroneously surmised. It was fortunate for Jeremy that he usually came up with an idea after going home and studying the meeting notes.

There was one thing Jeremy now knew with certainty: he hated his job. He could no longer stand it. Jeremy was firmly convinced of this when his eyes started dancing inside of his head. And dance they did. It started as a slow, seductive tarantella, his eyes moving with seemingly star-like ease through the gamut of styles. Then the tango, the waltz, the twist; at one point, his left eye was doing some kind of ballet, like a swoon, while his right eye was twerking in some kind of techno frenzy. His eyes collided behind his nose to create a spastic jitterbug, his entire head grabbing onto it with wild abandon. It felt as though his eyeballs had loosened from their sockets and were bugging through his brain.

He was brought back from all of this when he heard an insect buzzing around his head. He tried to swat at it, but the sound just got louder. Suddenly, as his mind gained more focus, Jeremy realized it wasn't a bug he heard, but the sound of someone saying his name.

"Stan? Stan?"

Good God, couldn't these people see he was in his *pose?* Of all the gall, this was the pose of impenetrability! This just could not happen. But it was.

"Stan, I really hate to bother you when you are so deep in thought, but we really need your input. The team is stuck. We were hoping you might have some insights to get us back on track."

With those words, Jeremy became completely unglued. He could no longer stand it. Out of the blue, a peculiar odor reached his nose. At first, he had no idea what it might be, as it was so out of place. As the smell grew stronger, it dawned on him what it was: WD-40. The smell continued to sharpen, and Jeremy mechanically rose to his feet. No, he was not Stan; this was not what his life was about. He'd be damned if he would die Stan Stanislaus.

Standing up bought Jeremy some time. He had no idea what he was going to say since he hadn't been listening. As he rose, no words came to his mind. However, the smell of WD-40 grew stronger with each passing second. The words "No more! No more!" began flashing red in his head, over and over again. Jeremy was now getting really anxious. Jeremy moved toward Dan, who was piloting the computer in this meeting. Jeremy figured he might create some pithy, cryptic slide to project, sending the rest of the team into a deep discussion and allowing him to slip out for the day. The voice in his head started up again. "You can't do this anymore!"

The smell of WD-40 intensified even more. Intermingled with it now was another smell. It was unmistakable. It was the smell of sweat. Sweat and muck. It was the smell of his dad. This was getting crazy.

As if he was being moved by remote control, Jeremy continued walking like a robot to the computer. He leaned over Dan and began typing. The phrase "Let's get funky!" appeared on the screen. As he straightened up, Jeremy realized he was grinning. The voice came back. "Don't just get funky, get goofy!"

A gurgle, more like a growl, came up from his throat. It exited his lips, as though he was a terrified squirrel. Before he knew it, he was on top of the table, bouncing and gyrating, his shoulders moving up and down at a frenetic pace. The dance in his head had progressed to his entire body. Jeremy was now lost in it all, dancing with frenetic joy, twerking and jerking in a way he had never done before and loving every moment of it.

In the middle of this exuberant dance-athon, Jeremy froze and surveyed the room, stuck mid-move. Stan's colleagues stared, open-mouthed, at him in terror. A few wore incredulous grins.

What had he just done? The voice came back again: "You are not Stan!"

Out. He had to get out — now.

Without warning, Jeremy began dancing again. His legs, arms, head, and torso were independently dancing to unique tunes he could not hear but surely must be playing. Suddenly he began scooting on his feet across the tabletop, his tiny stomach attempting to thrust itself forward as if initiating a belly thump with an invisible partner. Out of the corner of his eye he glimpsed door. He must look like a maniac to onlookers. It then occurred to Jeremy that he was, in fact, an actual maniac, convulsing on top of a table in the middle of a business meeting. He leapt over two colleagues, Irma and Neville, sitting across from him. Well, he guessed he wouldn't be asking Irma out any time soon, and there would be no more beers with Neville. His legs skimmed their heads as he flew over his stunned colleagues, then he hit the floor with his right leg and tumbled out the door.

Jeremy frantically looked around. It was as though it was the first time he had ever been in the hallway, as if he had somehow been dropped there out of the sky, or even transported to the hall by some invisible, alien hand. The fluorescent lights burned his eyes and made the hallway, with all its doors, seemingly throb and undulate around him, creating an eerie, iridescent brightness he had never noticed before but now was sure would choke him to death. The elevator — where was it? He had to get out now. If he didn't, Jeremy was sure something horribly wrong was going to happen. No, he couldn't take the elevator; it was too claustrophobic, especially if someone else was in there. Jeremy also realized he might have wet his pants, which would certainly make him poor company in the confines of an elevator. Maybe it was just sweat, he rationalized. No matter; whatever it was, sweat or pee, it was still gross.

Far down the hall he noticed a red exit sign looking larger than life. That was it: the stairs. He would use the stairs! A novel idea. He willed himself to run toward the door, but his legs no longer would listen to his brain. It was harder than it should have been, he thought, but he finally willed those appendages to move. Clumsily, Jeremy made his way toward the door as if he was waist-deep in mud. The sign was pulsing now — or was it just laughing at him? EXIT, EXIT, EXIT. No matter. He slogged onward, finally punching the metal handle of the door beneath the sign and lurching through the doorway, tripping and rolling down the set of stairs. He got to his feet and started running down the seventeen flights, sometimes hurdling over four or five steps at a time, holding the handrails to steady himself. When he finally made it to the door leading outside he pushed through it, crashing onto the street. He stopped for a moment to gather himself, look around, and assess the situation. Across the street from him, on top of a streetlamp, sat a crow — and right next to it sat a robin, calm and confident, obviously staring at

Jeremy. The fact was not lost on Jeremy that he had just minutes earlier been thinking about a robin.

Jeremy stood, transfixed for a moment. He had never seen anything quite like it; the juxtaposition of the two birds sitting beside each other was quite disarming. The robin stared, unmoving. Jeremy began to quickly walk toward the two birds. Out of his peripheral vision he saw movement. He turned towards it, only to be confronted by a car barreling toward him. Its driver appeared to be slamming on its brakes and it came to a stop just inches from his legs. He looked up again at the birds. The crow cawed. He swore he could see the robin nod its head his way.

An old man climbed out of the back of the car, a limousine, and beckoned Jeremy.

"You have the look of a man who could use a ride to the airport," he said with what sounded to be a slight British accent.

Short in stature with white hair and a white moustache, he opened the car's back door and waved at Jeremy again.

"Better hurry; that look you have on is as if you might miss your flight."

Jeremy moved toward the man, who took his arm and guided him toward the open door.

Before he bent his head to get in the car, Jeremy looked up. The birds were gone.

The elderly man slid into the seat beside Jeremy. Not knowing what to do, Jeremy decided that staring straight ahead and waiting might be a good initial strategy to buy him some time.

What the devil was going on? He had just run out of the building he worked in, or used to work in, leaving a prestigious job he thought he had wanted and had worked for years to get. Even though he was certain he would be labeled a raging lunatic in his chosen field, he felt remarkably relieved. Jeremy wasn't sure what had happened, what exactly had snapped, but he realized something he had known all along: This life was not for him, and now he was moving. Apparently Jeremy should go to the airport, and next to him sat a strange man who was using an incredibly affected British accent while employing a chauffeur decked out in a uniform and hat.

"Well, let's get you to the airport, young man," the old man said.

The airport — why the airport? He had nowhere to go, nobody to see. He finally turned and looked at the old gentleman.

"I certainly don't want to offend your privacy" — the old man said it in a bizarre way: priv-eh-si — "but you had the look of a man worried about missing a flight, so I had to stop. Let's get cracking, shall we, eh?"

Jeremy stared wide-eyed at the man.

"I will take that as a yes."

The man leaned toward the driver.

"Airport, Reginald. Departures."

Reginald nodded and the car accelerated at a frightening rate of speed.

Jeremy stared out the window. The car flew along at an incredible speed, swerving around cars, barely stopping at lights; he could see the terrified faces of pedestrians flash past.

"No dillydallying, Reginald, this man is obviously in a hurry."

Hurry?! Jeremy had no idea why he was in the car, why he was going to the airport, or why they were driving in such a way that would certainly kill them.

Moments ago, Jeremy repeated to himself, he had quit his job and danced the Watusi out of the building, screaming like a banshee and flaying as though he was on fire, and stumbled into this car with what appeared to be a wackadoodle old man and his chauffeur.

It had felt good, all that. It had actually felt wonderful, as though he had shed some reptilian skin, sloughing off dead epidermis that had been weighing him down for years. But now, settling back into a bit of uncomfortable reality, he became terrified at his new situation, and turned to glance at the old man who had been talking to him all the while. Jeremy raised his eyebrows slightly as he looked into the aged grey eyes. Everything about this man seemed to have a grey tinge to it. The man returned the glance.

"Ah, I surmise from the look you would like me to repeat that last bit, eh?"

Jeremy parted his lips as if to speak. Before he could, the old guy bulldozed on.

"Yes, well, to repeat — yes, back up a bit. What I was saying, now, was that some might just think it is a fantasy, a flaw if you will, that we as a human species, as it were, believe we actually have any clue what is really going on. I mean, take the orangutan, if you will; that lovely primate, who, in its natural state, glories and revels in the simplicity of . . ."

Jeremy lost the man's train of thought, just fell off the back of that train, and turned to look out the window. As he did, he saw an elderly woman dive backward away from the car, a look of terror on her face. He craned his neck backwards, watching her. She, thank God, appeared to be unscathed as she drifted out of sight. The car was still hurtling along, plowing down side streets and against traffic on one-way streets, but Jeremy wasn't certain where in town they were. The limo suddenly careened through a roundabout, which totally discombobulated him. At the third exit around the circle, tires screaming, they pulled onto a freeway on-ramp. This was certainly not a good thing, in Jeremy's mind, because Reginald apparently took the on-ramp as a green flag to move into warp speed. Jeremy turned to plead with the old man to tell Reginald to slow down, only to have the unflappable old geezer hold his hand up so he could finish his thought.

"And that is why it might be in our species' best interest to watch the beautiful orangutan more closely, even when they are placed in the direst of circumstances."

The old man leaned forward to the driver.

"It would mean a great deal to me if you could pick up the pace, Reginald, this young man has places to be."

Jeremy began to sputter. They were actually going to die. He was sure of it.

The old man stopped talking. He sat back in the seat and looked out the window for a time, stroking his face. Jeremy stared at him. There was something so familiar about him, but unfamiliar at the same time. Slowly the white head turned to Jeremy and looked at him. The way those kind grey eyes stared at Jeremy made him, somehow, relax. Jeremy could sense his breathing slowing, and he could no longer hear his heart banging away in his chest. The man reached out and patted his knee.

"It will be wonderful young man, you know, in the end."

Just as the man finished the words, the limo came to a screeching halt.

Reginald turned to the back seat. "Your gate, I believe."

He got out and opened the door for Jeremy. He didn't remember the car leaving the freeway; he didn't recall winding their way to the airport, to Departures, as the sign above informed him. Jeremy turned for the last time to look at the white-haired gentleman and thanked him — for what, he wasn't quite sure, but it seemed like the right thing to do. But the old guy appeared to be asleep, a slight smile peeking from behind his moustache.

Jeremy climbed out of the car. He looked up at Reginald, who winked at him as he slid back into the driver's seat. It was the first time Jeremy got a good look at old Reggie's face. Gnarled with deep, sunken eyes, a thick day-old beard, and tangled wrinkles, Reginald's face told Jeremy stories he could only imagine but knew were there. Reginald had on the strangest of smiles. It contained a mix of bemusement, whimsy, joy, and something else Jeremy couldn't quite put his finger on. One corner of Reggie's mouth was slightly upturned in a way so that it seemed as if he was sharing with Jeremy some kind of timeless joke.

Jeremy, however, wasn't quite sure what the joke was about.

Before he left, Reginald rolled his window down and looked at Jeremy in a way so as to let him know that, yes, even he knew it would be alright in the end. "Tut," was all Reginald had to say. The car sped off.

Jeremy stood there.

"Sir? Sir, you need to move. Excuse me."

Jeremy turned to face the enormous muscular chest of a huge man in a blue shirt and wearing a badge emblazoned with the words "Airport Police" on it. Jeremy slowly looked upward until he encountered a grinning face. It was a goofy grin; there was no other way to explain it.

The cop looked down on him, a smile covering his face. "You okay?"

Jeremy said nothing, looking quizzically into the enormous man's face.

"You okay?" he repeated. "Look, sorry, but you are slowing traffic and you're going to get hit. You have a flight?"

The officer gave a slight jerk of his head. Jeremy followed the direction of the jerk with his own head. Sure enough, the sign reading "Departures" was still there, looming over the cop's big blue shoulders. Jeremy moved his mouth to apologize, his jaw opening and closing like a carp on the shore gasping for air. He stumbled toward the doorway, lifting his hand in some kind of a weak, waving flutter, hoping that somewhere it communicated, "Sorry about that."

The officer called after him. "You be careful now."

Sure, sure, Jeremy would be careful. He was sure the man in blue had no idea he had spent most of his life trying to be careful, trying to predict what calamity might befall him next, always thinking about what might happen and then letting things happen because he was too busy thinking about what could happen tomorrow.

Once inside the terminal he immediately got caught up in the flow of travelers: people on the move, going nowhere, going somewhere. They were sad, excited, or both at once, heading on vacations, going to funerals, weddings, or on some very important business somewhere they just had to be.

The perplexing thing for Jeremy was that he wasn't one of them.

He shuffled along with the ocean of people because, quite honestly, it was the easiest thing to do. After a moment of lemminglike marching, he found himself slowing down out of no fault of his own. He realized he was in a line, moving toward a ticket counter. But he had no ticket to get, no place to go. The reader board with departing flights came into view: Orlando, Los Angeles, St. Louis, San Francisco.

San Francisco. Jeremy froze, staring at the name. His stare seemed to cross the crowd, to literally reach out and smash the words, which took him back to a family road trip many years earlier.

Suddenly, it seemed as though he was really there; a scared nine-year-old lying in the back of the 1958 baby blue Chevy station wagon his dad had bought and refurbished. Jeremy and Dwayne had thought he was crazy and loved to tease him when he wandered into the garage to work on the thing. The old man worked for months on that car. Jeremy would find the old man next to the station wagon, fiddling with something on it, completely lost in thought, smiling and humming. And one day it was done — new upholstery, the finish buffed out and waxed so that it gleamed. And he even made a little area in the "way back" of the car where Jeremy could stretch out and relax, a small bookshelf on the side for his things — screw the seatbelts.

"Just keep your head down when you're back there and nobody will notice," his dad had said. Dwayne's face tightened with worry for both himself and Jeremy, but he said nothing.

And then there he was, back in time. Not just a simple memory or daydream — Jeremy was there, now, in the back of the Chevy, driving through the redwoods. After the old man had fixed the thing, the three had decided they had to go somewhere in it, make an adventure, as it were. The family landed on San Francisco; the reason, though, was lost to the years.

But there Jeremy was, in the back of the wagon. He could smell the trees and the wet, damp soil and ferns that get so little sun with the redwood branches allowing just enough light to the forest floor for life to thrive. The smell was intoxicating and the enormity of the trees terrifying to Jeremy, yet beautiful at the same time. He lay down in the back of the car and watched the giant trees glide by. Little did Jeremy know at the time that while he was staring at them in the sky he was also driving over their network of roots that provide sustenance and create an interdependent web beneath the ground. Even those trees had community, a system of being. Looking at the sky and inhaling the vastness of it all brought him in and connected Jeremy to that web, as well. He could feel the moistness that inhabited the campsite where they relaxed for a few days, a calming quietness pervading their time there, even with the typical noises of the day that crowds of tourists brought with them...

Then he jumped in time to when they were crossing the Golden Gate Bridge on that same trip. The memory of the terror of crossing that spectacular structure came to him in full force. Certainly it was sheer craziness for anyone to build something like that — hanging over the water, reaching for the sky, crossing a void that had obviously been designed by the universe not to be crossed. At the same time, there was a grandness to it that had stuck with Jeremy. He had looked over the back seat to share his terror with his dad and Dwayne, to look for some comfort, but the two sat in the front seat, looking at the view, the old man whispering in awe to Dwayne.

"Can you believe it?"

Dwayne responded only by slightly nodding, his gaze transfixed out the passenger window toward the opening of the bay to the ocean. Jeremy slid back down onto his mat, suddenly not wanting to disturb the two. He closed his eyes and lay back down, waiting for it to end...

Apparently, the flight to San Francisco was uneventful, because Jeremy remembered nothing about it. In fact, when he opened his eyes, he was expecting to see the Golden Gate Bridge looming formidably over him; but, in fact, he was looking out the window of a plane, watching the runway come into view among the grey clouds. A flight attendant leaned over to make sure his seatbelt was fastened (Jeremy always kept his seatbelt buckled tightly across his lap when flying, unless he desperately needed to pee; did they think he was crazy? Who in their right mind invented tubes that fly through the air, crammed with people, going hundreds of miles an hour?) and welcomed him to San Francisco, so he knew he had somehow bought a ticket and boarded a flight. Jeremy congratulated himself for at least picking a place he liked.

He grabbed a cab to the wharf, born from a lack of having anywhere else to go as opposed to wanting to go there, and found a small hotel. As he checked in, the desk clerk asked if he'd like help with his bags. Realizing for the first time he *had no bags*, Jeremy declined and embarrassedly retreated to his room. He sat there for a bit, trying to get his bearings and wondering what he should do next or what might happen next. After a quick trip to the store for some clean clothes and a toothbrush, he ventured into the streets of San Francisco and headed to the North Beach neighborhood. Wandering past the strip clubs, bookstores, and restaurants, Jeremy came upon a small old hotel. A soothing light emanated out its windows and onto the sidewalk where he stood. He looked inside at the mustard walls and could hear the sound of slow jazz and smell the delicious scent of roasting garlic wafting from the building. Through the window he could see the restaurant patrons talking to each other across the table. They appeared to be familiar locals (at least from the way they dressed): affluent old-school San Franciscans enjoying a meal, music, and community.

Looking to find an entrance, an image appeared in the front window. It was quite a bizarre image. *Oh God, what was happening now?* It took a moment, but Jeremy soon realized it was his image he was staring at. You see, he had forgotten he'd quickly picked up some things to wear at a store close to his hotel. Jeremy's clothes were two days old and had been, along with his person, through quite a bit of trauma. To put it bluntly, they stank. The convenience store by the hotel had little to offer; the best he could find was a ready-made steampunk closeout Halloween costume. once back in his room he had peeled off the stuff that had affixed itself to his body, not bothering to look at his new ensemble. When he saw it in the package, a white shirt, bow tie, shiny black pants, and faux straw bowler hat seemed pretty sedate. He'd thrown on the hat due to the drizzle when he left his room, and now, looking into the old hotel, the reflection staring back at him was, well, interesting to say the least. Seeing as he was hungry, he tucked the hat under his arm, combed his hair with his fingers, and headed into the restaurant. The sheer smells of the Italian food, along with amicable chatter, brought back memories of home, pasta, dad, and Dwayne.

The maître d' raised an eyebrow as Jeremy entered. Would she even seat him? Was there an open table? Jeremy forgot he was in San Francisco. Without a word, the woman tilted her head and led him to a small table in a corner. No one seemed to notice as they glided by; rather, the guests' earnest conversations continued without missing a beat. No sooner had Jeremy sat down than a waiter appeared with a glass of white wine, which would turn out to be one of the best glasses of chardonnay he had ever tasted, and some warm olives and freshly baked bread.

Over the next two hours the meal that came to him, each course coming at the exact moment he had started to miss the last plate and was wondering what would come next, was one that Jeremy knew would never be forgotten. Most memorable of all in the epicurean extravaganza was a linguine con funghi like no other Jeremy had ever tasted before. During the meal, the soothing sounds of a jazz combo floated through the room and eased his spirit. He hadn't noticed an older woman until, after a time, she rose from a table off to the side and made her way to a microphone. Slight and regal, the room fell silent as she began to sing, her voice deep and throaty. Jeremy immediately lost himself in the song and the aura that emanated from her.

> *Winds blow,*
> *Gently pushing through the night.*
> *Your smile remains among the clouds,*
> *Not in my memory*
> *But here and now and always.*
> *Forevermore, forevermore,*
> *Time recedes as the sun rises,*
> *Forevermore, forevermore.*

The woman finished to polite applause. Before returning to her seat, she wandered among the other patrons, chatting and offering hugs. She never made it to his corner of the room.

Done with his meal and sitting with a half-sipped glass of port, it dawned on Jeremy that it felt as if he was in a bubble. It seemed to Jeremy that no one had noticed him during his entire meal, and the faint conversations that drifted his way never quite made it to his brain. After a bit, Jeremy rose, wandering out as if he was invisible, and ambled back to his hotel.

He sat up in bed with a jolt. The bill. He had forgotten to pay the bill at the restaurant. No one had approached him as he left, and it simply slipped his mind. He looked at the clock; it was after three o'clock in the afternoon! Jeremy quickly called his front desk so that he could retrieve the clothes he had sent out to be cleaned, only to find they weren't back yet. He threw the costume back on and headed back to the restaurant to pay his bill and apologize profusely. He made a brisk walk of it back to North Beach, only to find the place missing. Or rather, not there. The hotel was there, appearing much older than he had remembered, but there was no fancy restaurant. No delicious smells, no quaint tables, no enchanting music. Nothing but a small, completely bland hotel cafe.

Jeremy wandered into the lobby, past the desk clerk, through a gift shop area, and into the restaurant. The maître d' from the night before was there, prepping at the front, folding napkins. He stood before her, expecting to get an earful about the unpaid bill. Nothing. Finally, she looked up at him.

"Hello, may I help you?"

Jeremy stared.

"Is there something I can do for you? Is there something you need?"

He didn't know what to say.

"We're not open yet; if you want a table, you'll need to wait a bit. And we're pretty booked tonight, so it will be a while."

He stared imploringly at the woman. She didn't recognize him.

Jeremy tried to speak but it was a garbled mess. He was so confused.

"I'm afraid I don't understand, sir."

That couldn't be. The people, the delicious food. The music, the woman singing.

A pause. The two looked at each other.

"You okay?" she asked. "Need some help?"

Jeremy looked around again, hoping that some crazy derelict had entered behind him. No, she was talking to him. He didn't know what to do; he couldn't speak and was too embarrassed to run. He realized now he couldn't move if he wanted to. His eyes began to twitch back and forth. In his periphery he noticed a clothing rack and quickly grabbed a sweatshirt. Yes, he would buy something, that might help things a bit. The words "Hotel Renaldo" were emblazoned on the front. He slipped it over his head — backwards, it turned out — stuffed his hands in his pockets, pulled out a wad of cash, tossed some clumsily on the counter, and bolted for the door. Out in the street he could hear her call after him.

"Hey, don't you want your change?"

Thank God he'd paid enough. He hurried off down the street — she could keep the extra money for her trouble.

Here he was, running again, scurrying off to nowhere in particular, but needing to move, move somewhere, be somewhere he could rest, be comfortable in his skin for just even a bit and collect his thoughts. Maybe he ought to take a cab back to the airport. Go home; well, not home, but his apartment. He realized he really had no home; hadn't had one since he left what had been his home with Dwayne and the old man.

He heard seagulls behind him. Slowly he turned around, and there, in an alley, were a group of gulls pecking away at a dumpster full of garbage. He looked closer among the gulls rifling through the goodies in a black garbage bag. Up popped the damn robin again. It looked directly at Jeremy. Their eyes locked. Then the bird flew off. The gulls watched as the robin left, glanced at Jeremy, squawked, and departed in the same direction. Jeremy was feeling increasingly uneasy. He turned away from the alley and was transported back in time. There he was again, sitting in the old truck with his dad. The old man turned to him, smiling, and said, as he often did when they went driving, "We got nowhere to go today, buddy. And nowhere to go when we get back from there." He laughed a big belly laugh and his image disappeared. That seemed to be the story of his life right now, Jeremy thought: nowhere to go. The wharf — he could smell the wharf. It was time to follow the bird.

Jeremy headed toward the waterfront and wandered along the wharf, past the inane gift shops, vendors, fortune tellers, and hawkers trying to get him on an excursion boat to Alcatraz. Occasionally he was sure he caught someone out of the corner of his eye doing a double take upon looking at him. He must have looked a sight given what he was wearing: the plastic bowler, hotel sweatshirt on backwards, and shiny black pants. Still, it was San Francisco — wasn't he *underdressed?* No matter, he now felt he was on a mission. What for, he wasn't sure. Maybe it just was what it was: a mission to nowhere. He upped his pace. He had to get there, wherever that might be. When he reached his destination, the destination being the water for the fact that he could go no further, he stopped and leaned on a railing, looking out on the piers jutting out of the water, creating a foundation for the wharf's restaurants to lure tourists.

Settling against the railing, Jeremy saw a large family was to his right, feeding crumbs to the gulls from a loaf of bread. There appeared to be quite a few insatiable seagulls hanging out. As his breathing calmed down a bit, Jeremy thought of all that had happened in the last twenty-four hours. Relief and joy, things he had not felt in quite a long time, crept over him. Jeremy had hated that job, he now realized. The job itself certainly had no idea what the term joy meant; the tension, lack of meaning, purpose with no meaning. He had strived for what he thought the world defined as happiness. But no, it was a cruel joke. Thoughts of the previous evening came back to mind: the pure sensory delight and knowing no future at the moment and no past, it all melded into a series of moments both past and future — not an image, but a feeling. The people in the restaurant the night before appeared as if out of time, existing in that state for eternity. From there, images of the past emerged, but not memories; rather, something more potent: feelings, smells, a sense of being. The feeling of the blanket in Dwayne's attic refuge the day he had crashed his bike. Good God, the bike and his old man's intensity and absorption as he worked on a child's bike. The world seemed to disappear when the guy was working on something.

The present reappeared. Something, or someone, was staring at him, Jeremy could feel it. Glancing over, a very large seagull was watching him. It made Jeremy a bit uncomfortable. The family who had been feeding the gulls was gone, but the birds were not. Jeremy realized it was not just the ginormous gull that was staring at him, but *all* of them. At *him*, Jeremy was sure of it. In unison, or so it seemed, they hopped a bit closer, and then a bit closer. Jeremy stepped back, and they countered with another hop. He was sure he could hear a "thump" when they landed. This continued: a step back, a hop forward. Jeremy was quite alarmed.

He turned and scurried away from them — let some other tourists deal with the hungry mob. Heading toward the Embarcadero, he glanced over his shoulder. The bird army had turned en masse and were marching silently after him. Jeremy picked up his pace. Another quick glance left no doubt that they were following. Some were flying overhead, but a growing host of seagulls was advancing on foot behind him. People were starting to stare, he was sure of it. Jeremy turned and began walking at a fast clip. Jeremy couldn't say for sure, since he hadn't wanted to slow down and take a look, but it certainly seemed as though, out of the blue, one of the more obstreperous ones bit him on the butt.

That was it; they were after him. He began to run. Jeremy could hear them, feel them following, and he took off as if — and at that moment he thought it did — his life depended on it. For some inexplicable reason he began to worry that his hat might come off, the plastic dome he'd bought the prior night, so he clamped a hand down on it. He could hear it crack. He pushed it harder onto his head. He was now sprinting down the sidewalk toward the Embarcadero, his breath becoming more labored and his legs tiring. Looking behind him one more time was a huge mistake, as there seemed to be hundreds of birds now, most marching toward him on the ground, some flying low beside him, and others squawking overhead. And then it happened, he felt a splat on the hand holding down his hat. *Gull crap.* Jeremy could hear and see it hitting the ground around him as well as feel the direct hits. People were now scurrying out of the way, taking pictures and laughing.

Jeremy was getting tired but, too scared to stop, he had no idea what to do. Up ahead was a building: Pier 27, the sign read. Where the sidewalk split he saw a path that led toward the water. At the intersection was a large, life-sized cutout of a nun wearing a captain's hat. In her outstretched hand was a sign with an arrow pointing toward a ship and the wording "Free cruise ship tours. Get a glimpse of the good life aboard the Paternoster of the Sea." The nun saluted invitingly with her free hand. Jeremy kicked his speed into overdrive and sprinted toward the craft. The gangway came into view. He glanced at the ship and, upon seeing its name for the second time, emblazoned on the bow, he realized what an odd name Paternoster of the Sea was for a cruise ship.

Stepping aboard, Jeremy turned to see if, as his innermost fears portended, he would need to engage in mortal combat with the mighty host of seagulls. Hundreds of them stood in the pavilion in front of the ship, staring at him. Jeremy stared back. As a group, the gulls turned and began marching off, some flying away and others wandering off, looking for tourists to get a free snack from. The few other tour goers on the ship had not seemed to notice the interaction, and Jeremy took a deep breath to try and relax a bit. He looked down the deck. Before he could exhale, he saw him. Standing along the railing, with a seagull on his shoulder, was the old man who took him to the airport. Jeremy froze. The old gentleman turned and winked at Jeremy. Jeremy made a quick 180-degree turn, and there she was, the woman who had been singing the night before, feeding seagulls. She turned and gave a little wave. Spooked to distraction, Jeremy had no idea what to do. Quickly, he turned on his heel, deciding his best course of action was to run into the ship and hide. Hide for a bit and cower, collect his thoughts, stop the racing mind, slow the breathing down, get a little focus. He was at his wit's end. At no time in his memory had he wished more for presence of mind or for someone to confide in — Dwayne or, God he missed him, Dad.

He began to run for the doorway, then smacked into a real-life nun; a very big and tall nun with enormous breasts. He head-planted into the gargantuan orbs, his nose smashing directly into a wooden crucifix that hung between them. He had never been very religious, and he didn't think for a minute that God was planning on saving him now. His dad and uncle never much mentioned the whole affair; instead, they always focused on the here and now, the moment, so it seemed, letting the universe guide, direct, and offer them comfort when they asked.

He looked up. Looking down at him with the goofiest grin he had ever seen, and he had seen a few in last two days, was a full-fledged nun alright, donned from head to toe in a black-and-white habit. She smiled down at him, showing two missing front teeth.

"Go with God," she said, and gave him a pat on the head.

And that was it. Jeremy left the building, or his body, so to speak. He didn't exactly lose consciousness, and he didn't pass out. The best description was that a piece of him began to float. It went nowhere in particular, but his mind, his being, just floated away. He certainly wasn't dead; he somehow knew that for sure. He could feel his body, in a weird way, but he did know that he wasn't in it. In a whirlwind of darkness things came to him — not like in a dream, not images in his head, but in his very being. He could feel, smell, and see things in a way he had ever experienced. The past, present, and, yes, the future were all there at once. It was a mass of sensory explosion, with all senses and emotions melding together at once. A purple color, or feeling, permeated everything, and moments of time began vividly erupting. He was eating in his kitchen with his family, then riding his bike that fateful day he smashed into Mr. What's-His-Name's car and met the robin for the first time. Then Jeremy saw himself as an old man, tending to something in the ground while a small child sitting next to him had her arm around the strangest dog he had ever seen. And then there was a woman's face looking tenderly at him. It was his mother, he knew that; although he had no real memory of her, for some reason he knew it was her. Finally, he saw another woman's face, one he had never seen awake or dreaming, and the most intense feeling he had ever experienced overcame him. His being melted into her.

With that loss of identity among the swirling, an overwhelming feeling of calm came through, telling him it was okay, that everything would be okay, as he had been told, and as it should be. It seemed for a moment as if he was folding into himself. And then, inside it all, he began to feel as if he were becoming a whole person again. Jeremy was no longer scattered higgledy-piggledy all over the universe and across time, not second guessing who he was or should be, but just Jeremy, a changed Jeremy, with new pieces coming together with the old.

From there, back in his body again, he drifted about the ship. He could see a large pavilion and floated through it, bumping into a wall before gliding into the grand ballroom. The old man who had given him the ride to the airport and the woman who had been singing, both who he had seen moments earlier, were there, as well as others who had helped him recently. There was Reginald, the driver, who sat at a table sipping something. He nodded as Jeremy floated by. The woman singer waved to him again. Scattered about the room were other faces he recognized, but wasn't sure from where. After seeing several people he thought he knew it dawned on him that they were people who had, at some time in his life, done a kindness for him. Some folks he had never met, but he somehow felt he had known them for a very long time. Or perhaps would know them someday. It made him feel safe and connected. On the wall was a giant mural depicting people in a green field, dancing, sitting on blankets, enjoying themselves. Many of the faces scattered throughout the mural looked familiar, but Jeremy couldn't quite place them. One gentleman, sitting on a blanket wearing black pants, a white shirt, and a bow tie, staring right at him, looked remarkably like his father. One thing was certain: everyone in the picture looked quite content. In the center of the picture were two figures dancing together, leaning backward and laughing joyously. Jeremy focused on the couple who was in such carefree abandon. His brain began to process the two figures, the gears of his mind and memory making the connection — it was a big-bellied laughing Buddha and his partner. His partner was not familiar to Jeremy. She was laughing with her head back and arms open, dressed in robes that seemed to change color as he passed the mural. The feeling that came from watching her was one of wonder, joy and awe; she was someone you just wanted to be near to experience their presence. As he kept walking past, he swore her lips moved and that she spoke directly to him. "Remember this," was what he thought she mouthed. Boy, was she having a good time. Everything was as it should be.

Suddenly, an explosion of light crashed through his being. Cascading joy overcame him, and then he felt nothing. Jeremy was in a void.

Jeremy had no idea how long he slept or, to be more precise, for how long he was dead to the world. He slept the dark, peaceful slumber that comes from total exhaustion and emotional fatigue. Occasionally he could sense himself touching a bit of consciousness; so, thankfully, he wasn't dead, but for the most part he was gone to the world. Wakefulness came in a slow, wavelike manner, soothing and at the same time invigorating. Reality came incrementally, in no hurry. Taking stock of his surroundings, Jeremy could tell he was in bed, a soft, cozy, delightful, and warm cocoon. Lying motionless, eyes closed, he felt the way he always should. He stayed that way for a very long time, or so it seemed. Slowly, Jeremy allowed his eyes to open. He was in a large stateroom, facing a window that opened to a balcony. Still on the ship, or so it appeared, as he could tell his accommodation was moving through the water. It didn't matter. Looking about, the room was a simple affair: a set of clothes hung on a hook on what must be the door to a bathroom, and on a small table was a tray with a tiny loaf of brown bread, a bowl of fruit, a carafe of water, and a pot of tea waving invitingly at him. The smell and beautiful way the food was arranged made him realize he was ravenously hungry. Slipping on the comfortable linen pants and shirt, he gathered the tray and brought it back to the warm comfort of the bed and had a taste. Though simple, it was truly delicious: warm moist brown bread and butter, fresh fruit like nothing he had had before, and sweet floral tea. He finished the meal, watching the sky grow dark and the moon and stars emerge to greet the evening.

There Jeremy sat. It came to his mind that, in times of great pain and fear, sitting and letting his mind empty of thought seemed to bring comfort. The horizon peacefully passed by as his mind rested and he let it empty out. He was still frightened, good God, with what was going on in his life, but he felt that however it turned out, it was going to be okay. Thoughts came to his mind during this time, but then gently floated away. Back into mind came the who-knows-how-long-ago time he had spent in the basement of the old house after his dad left the planet. He somehow found peace in that thought, and those feelings came back tenfold as he looked out the window at the moonshine dancing on the water. And so Jeremy, for Stan was dead and gone forever, sat. Time disappeared.

When thinking began again, slowly at first, and the felt present of the room returned, Jeremy noticed the sky was beginning to warm with color. Dawn emerged in unique and beautiful increments, and those moments between dark and dawn filled the room and his soul. He sat transfixed as a feeling like no other resonated through him. Slowly, light crept into the world, and with it came a robin, probably *the* robin. How in the world it had managed the journey was a curiosity in itself. Had it been there all along? If it ever left him was a question which Jeremy was not sure of the answer, nor did it matter. There it sat, on the balcony, facing west, with the horizon slowly glowing a deep orange from the sun rising in the east.

There was a slight knock at the door. Jeremy sat still, not wanting the moment to end. The bird slowly turned so it was facing Jeremy, looking at him in an odd yet familiar and knowing way. Where had he seen those eyes before?

"Don't you think you ought to get that?" Jeremy's head filled with the words, the thought resonating in his brain. He was mildly amused that he felt no fear or surprise; had this happened before he had boarded the ship, he would have been looking for a place to hide. He knew it came from the bird.

"Ah, finally listening, I see. Thank goodness. I knew you'd come around someday."

The two exchanged a long, thoughtful stare.

"Be seeing you." Off it flew.

Upon opening the stateroom's door, Jeremy found yet a new meal was laid out on a little cart. A large, gift-wrapped box had been laid on a shelf underneath it. Wheeling the contraption in, Jeremy examined this morning's breakfast. It had the same foods as the last meal, and that was good news. As simple as the previous meal had been, it was one of the most delectable meals he had ever had, and he was once again hungry. He poured some tea, tore off a small piece of bread, and slowly chewed it as he examined the box and placed it next to him on the bed. He sat there contentedly, savoring the simple meal. He could not believe how delicious the simple fare tasted.

On top of the box was a card that read "From the Gang." As he started to open the gift, Alice's words as she entered Wonderland came to mind: it was getting "curiouser and curiouser!" Lifting the lid and examining the contents, Jeremy smiled. From the perspective of an outside observer, most of the happenings of the last week (or so it seemed) could be attributed to the overactive imagination of someone who couldn't stand their job, hated their life, so snapped a bit and went off on a wild tangent, probably fueled by alcohol. Jeremy knew this was not the case. He decided it was time to enjoy the ride; there was no sense in allowing terror to run the show. The box contained durable clothes: some brown sturdy pants, a T-shirt, a light sweater, a duster jacket, and some stout-looking walking shoes. At the bottom of the box sat an oilskin sou'wester. It looked like somebody was expecting weather.

The ship had changed course and was heading a bit to the east. Still no land was in view, but something was happening, and Jeremy figured he had better put the clothes on, as they weren't some forgotten birthday gift that had finally arrived. They'd been delivered for a reason; he was sure of that. After showering and getting cleaned up and dressed properly for the first time since the day he had quite unceremoniously quit his job, land could be seen through the window. As to where it was, that remained a mystery.

No sooner had he finished getting dressed than three loud knocks hit the door. He turned and stared, not sure what to do. Three knocks again, this time louder, and then the frightening howl of a dog. Or wolf. Or coyote. Or rabid banshee. Jeremy caught himself and smiled, remembering he had just solemnly promised himself to enjoy the ride.

"How a' ye?" The deep voice of a man came out in a singsong voice from the other side of the door. "I do, I do, be knowin' yer in, I do. Ye gots ta open the door. Ye gots ta."

There wasn't much else to do. Jeremy slowly walked to the door and opened it a crack, surprised by his own lack of terror. He could smell him first: wood smoke, an earthy odor, and something not unpleasant but kind of musky. It suddenly came to him — wet dog. Glancing through the crack in the door, he saw a pair of round, twinkling eyes. The eyes and the head gave a slight bow. Jeremy looked down, only to see the same twinkling eyes nestled into a dog's face. The dog bowed as well.

"Howdy, howdy be doodly doody."

Beyond the first set of eyes was a wrinkled forehead and a few strands of wiry black-and-grey hair protruding from a strange, floppy, wide-brimmed black hat. Opening the door a bit further out of curiosity, Jeremy saw that a giant grin rounded out the face. A happy, silly grin. Jeremy's skin tingled. Nervously, as he did not really want to, Jeremy shifted his gaze downward. At about navel level were the two eyeballs he had quickly glanced at, still attached to an enormous dog's face, which was complete with an enchanting grin and tongue lolling out of its mouth. The rest of the pooch was skinny and gangly, with hair similar to the man's — but lots of it, sticking out every which way.

"Howdy be doody."

Jeremy opened the door further and backed into the room. Although exceedingly out of the ordinary, the two appeared benign and, if they were not, Jeremy could make a break for the window and swim for safety. Into the room wandered the man and the dog, which was the strangest species he had ever seen.

The man was over six feet tall, skinny, and his arms and legs dangled about as if the ligaments and muscles weren't quite attached enough to his body. He indeed wore a large black hat that was flat on the top with an enormous brim flopping wildly about when he moved. Shoulder-length hair sprouted out of the brim of the hat, framing a giant craggy face with a pointy nose. The most amazing and endearing aspect of him was that he sported the most welcoming, mischievous, and infectious grin Jeremy had ever seen. Slowly looking down, Jeremy again assessed the dog, which was pretty much a dog version of the man, but without the hat, and the dog's grin beat the man's, hands down. Its long wet tongue made the creature even more lovable. Jeremy's fear disappeared and was replaced by curiosity and a quickly growing affection.

Jeremy stared at the two. The two stared back. Jeremy was transfixed. Suddenly, the dog let out a howl.

"Aaaaarrrrooooooooooo."

"What, you ain't ne'er be seein' a lurcher befor'? I do believ' yer embarrassin' her, I do."

The dog howled again, then jumped on Jeremy and licked his face. The man didn't say a word about it.

"Baz McDooney. Pleasure, sir."

There was a pause.

"An' yer dog's nem be Lucy."

Baz stuck out his spindly hand. The dog raised her paw.

Not knowing what else to do and not wanting to be rude, Jeremy shook both and then stared at the dog in disbelief.

"Oh, she be yers alrigh', alrigh', thet's fer sure, to be sure." There was another long pause and then he said, "Look boy, we gots ta be gettin'. People be waitin'."

Baz turned toward the door. Lucy sat and stared at Jeremy, her tail wagging and tongue lolling around. Jeremy looked out the window. The boat was indeed stopping. Jeremy and Lucy stared at each other for a moment. Lucy gently licked Jeremy's hand and sat back and stared at him with a look of love and adoration that melted his heart. She had his back for eternity. With that understanding, the two headed out of the room after Baz. Why not? With a dog like Lucy by your side, you could dance through the gates of hell.

As they headed down the empty hall, Jeremy smiled. He might as well see where this adventure leads. It appeared as though he now owned a dog, it sounded as though "people" were waiting, plus Baz was so thoroughly likable.

Baz picked up his pace, adding a little skip to his step, and began to sing in a deep baritone voice.

> *Ah, the dawn is kinda scary*
>
> *Because it brings about the light*
>
> *And all the creepy woobly things*
>
> *Come out to their delight.*
>
> *And the dusk is really nasty*
>
> *Because it throws you in the dark,*
>
> *And who knows what might come out*
>
> *And scare you for a lark.*
>
> *Yes, the world's a scary place,*
>
> *There isn't any doubt,*

So why not do a little dance

And buss it on the snout?

When Baz hit the word "doubt" he jumped and kicked his heels together. Lucy, walking beside Jeremy, kicked up her hind legs and gave a little "woof" right after. When the song, as it were, ended, Lucy let out what appeared to Jeremy be her signature howl: "Aaaaar-rrrooooooooooo."

"She do love that one, she do. Remember it. Want me ta sing it again?" Baz turned back and gave Jeremy a wink. Jeremy politely shook his head. They continued down the long hallway. Baz and Lucy kept up a chatter all the way: Baz talking about the impending weather, rain, and other mundane topics, and the lurcher responding with the oddest of dog talk. At one point there was a brief pause in the chatter, and Lucy made a series of sounds that could only be recognized in the form of a question.

"I know ye want cheese, I do know. That be, it be fer him ta decide."

Lucy let out a series of low howls.

"Yes, I know, I know ye want Camembert, but it gives ye gas, it does. And 'tis foul."

A low growl sounded. Lucy stopped and sat down. Jeremy stopped. She lifted her paw and Jeremy took it, not sure what else to do.

Baz looked at Jeremy. "Now she's embarrassed." Then, to Lucy, he said, "I'm sorry, but it do be foul. And he's gonna find out sooner or later."

Yes, it was true: Jeremy now had a dog.

They came to the hallway's exit. Jeremy could feel the cool, moist air through the open doorway. It was cloudy. No one was around. Since they had left the room, Jeremy had not seen another person. It was if the ship was empty; he had not seen even a crew member, yet it was moored at the dock. It dawned on him suddenly — was this created just for him? How in the world could that be?

Baz stepped aside for Jeremy and Lucy to pass him. They walked down the gangway. Jeremy could feel Lucy nuzzling and licking his hand occasionally. About halfway down, the two stopped and turned towards Baz to see if he was going to usher in what was next.

Baz was gone.

Jeremy looked down at Lucy. She stood staring and smiling at him, tail wagging. She started to talk at him, mumbling a bit and fidgeting, as if trying to get him to move. They interacted like this for a time, and Jeremy could feel Lucy's presence trying to open him up, as if reaching inside and touching his heart. Their eyes melted together. Jeremy realized that he didn't have a dog; rather, Lucy had a human, and had just attached herself to him in a way that could never be broken. A wave of comfort and calm passed through him as he smiled down at this amazing creature. Finally, he turned with her and they continued down the gangway. On the shore, a few yards from the ship, stood someone in a duster like the one Jeremy was wearing. Lucy trotted towards the figure. She approached the man and he knelt down to scratch her. Jeremy got closer and the figure stood up.

It was Uncle Dwayne.

He stared across the grass at Uncle Dwayne. Jeremy wasn't sure exactly where he was, though he could make a good guess. Wherever he was, there was Dwayne, waiting for him. He wondered how long his uncle had been here; Jeremy hadn't seen him in at least ten years. The two stared at each other. Dwayne raised an eyebrow and smiled.

"Here so soon. We knew you'd start listening someday, but I didn't think it would happen so fast." There were the enigmatic first words that came from Dwayne. "So glad you met Baz. He said a dog arrived for you the other day, so I knew you were on your way. Sweet puppy. And as for Baz, we will see him again sometime, be sure about that."

The gears in Jeremy's mind started turning faster and faster. But instead of spiraling into unfounded conjecture and anxiety this time, the gears slowed and a bit of clarity began to seep in. Not complete understanding, mind you, but clarity just the same. It somehow was all connected — that was becoming apparent. Not just the past few days but all his life, and he knew now he wasn't just imagining it. And what in the world did Dwayne and his dad have to do with it? The words from his father the day he died came back to Jeremy: "Things are seldom as they seem." The robin from his childhood, seen first that fateful day with the bike that appeared with Dwayne's words, the strange occurrences throughout his life, even his father's demise at that precise time in his life now all seemed interconnected. The meltdown in the conference room, leading to the obliteration of his career, had somehow blown a door wide open, and from that opening some very remarkable, if not strange, things were cascading out. He looked down at Lucy, who was wagging her tail, tongue hanging out.

She gave him a goofy grin and licked his hand. She was talking alright, and he was beginning to listen.

Jeremy looked at Dwayne, who smiled back. Many questions, and a bit of anger, came rushing to his head. He'd been abandoned, hadn't he? As quickly as they had come, though, the frightening thoughts drifted into oblivion. Dwayne's smile, his presence, was what was important. Who knew what he had gone through? None of that mattered suddenly. Words didn't matter. The three of them turned together and wandered along the bluff. A few miles off the shore huge mountains emerged from the sea. Jeremy stared out and placed his hand on Lucy's head. She nuzzled his leg. He could hear Dwayne sigh. Home — he felt at home for the first time in years.

Reacquainting with Dwayne, as it were, didn't happen the way Jeremy initially expected. The two didn't go someplace and spend hours or days catching up on life and their respective experiences that had brought them to this precise place. Questions about where Dwayne had been and why he had disappeared didn't seem to matter anymore. No, they walked along the water and through streets for days, the three of them. Through their wanderings of the coastal town, a catching up occurred in its own way: in silence, mostly. Conversation got in the way. Feeling calm and almost surreal, Jeremy felt his anxiety and fear receding, and breathing came like he was learning it all over again. The air was clean and sweet, even in the torrential rain, and filled him with wonder. As for Dwayne, it seemed his experiences had drained his nervousness and constant worry to a trickle. The Dwayne from the day after Jeremy crashed his bike, when he brought him tea, was all that remained, only stronger, more assured, and definitely at peace.

A room was waiting for Jeremy in Dwayne's tiny house nestled in the trees by the water. During his initial time with Dwayne, it was the process of living that Jeremy remembered, not the events. Realizing the life he had led the past decade was about nothing more than building walls in an effort to stop the waves of angst that constantly battered him was freeing. During this time, it began to become apparent to him that those walls had prevented him from sensing that a reality existed that was unlike anything he had imagined and was so much more than anything he had ever known. As the robin had pointed out to him, he began to listen; to listen in a way he had never known possible. Jeremy stopped using just his ears and began learning to listen with his entire being.

With all that swirling around in his mind, Jeremy addressed his new life. It was hard at times and confusing. He relished this time with Dwayne. He lived his life for a time, walking, enjoying the world and his uncle's company, and cooking. Jeremy came to realize he loved to cook as much as his father and Dwayne had, and cooking meals together, providing feasts for newfound friends, became Jeremy's delight.

So it came as a shock when Jeremy woke one night filled with terror, frightened by a dream he could not recall. It left him with a feeling of being terribly alone and afraid. After getting his bearings, Jeremy looked down at a wide-awake Lucy staring at him, her head on his stomach. She was panting, a paw resting on his chest as if in an effort to calm him. He stared at his best friend, reflexively stroking her head in an effort to relax and gently breathe. Thoughts rushed into his mind. Perhaps he could try to get his old job back? If he groveled enough and agreed to go into therapy maybe he would be allowed back into that world. He knew instinctively this was crazy talk, as going back to the world of tall buildings and meaningless tasks would the death of his soul, but he couldn't shake the questions from his mind.

Jeremy heard jars opening and pots clanking in the kitchen. Dwayne was up to something. A few minutes later his uncle appeared in the bedroom doorway, holding two cups of his signature calming tea. Dwayne came in and handed Jeremy a cup before sitting down, silently, on the end of the bed. The two nodded at each other, sipping their drinks. There they sat, a sense of calm slowly coming back to Jeremy a bit.

"Fear got ahold of you again, eh?" Dwayne began. After what seemed like a very long time, Dwayne continued. "You know what happened to you on the Paternoster, don't you."

It wasn't so much of a question, but more of an affirmation.

Jeremy looked at Dwayne. Lucy stayed sprawled across Jeremy, gazing at him.

The next part of the conversation stayed with Jeremy for the rest of his life. He was never sure if Dwayne had spoken the words, or if they had just magically appeared in Jeremy's brain.

"My dear lad, you are special — as we all are. But you have overcome your fears of the world remarkably quickly in your short life. What you must try to comprehend is that the universe is rooting for you in a very big way. You are here for some purpose, Jeremy.

Perhaps it is just being that: Jeremy. You are developing inner talents some work a lifetime to merely comprehend or barely grasp. Your experience in that office of yours might have given you, upon reflection, an idea that something was moving you forward, giving you a nudge. The odor that permeated the room in that dreadful place wasn't just your overactive imagination. Don't believe that for a second."

At that, Dwayne stood, put his teacup on the bedside table, and patted Jeremy on the knee. Lucy immediately hopped off the bed and trotted to the house's front door. Dwayne followed, grabbing his coat and wandering out the door with Lucy. Then they turned toward Jeremy, waiting.

Jeremy scrambled out of bed, setting his cup on the quilt, putting the wheels in motion to have gravity pull it over; for it to be there all over the bedsheets when he returned. Jeremy hopped after them, clumsily donning his pants and coat.

The group walked off the porch and headed to their favorite spot at the water. There the three stood and looked out over the water in silence. A deep orange moon hung in the horizon like a neon sign, telling them the universe was open for business. The bright myriad of stars seemed to dance, their reflection on the water making it appear as though the three were immersed in infinity. The two men stood shoulder to shoulder and Lucy lay atop their feet. They stood this way in silence for a very long time, letting the magic soak in. Slowly, ever so slightly, Jeremy could feel himself and the world around him dissolve. It was not completely unlike his experience on the ship, but this time it happened gradually, until he felt as though he had once again ceased to exist as a singular entity. The strange part was that, with the dissolution, he felt as though he existed everywhere. As this happened, he could sense pieces of others like him mingling in it all.

The whole thing abated the same way it had begun, slowly and gradually, until he was back, looking at the water. The three were motionless, enjoying the moonlight. Dwayne began speaking again.

"We accept the fact that an invisible force keeps our planet circling around the sun with all of us affixed to it. Gravity is not questioned. Yet the energy we just felt, coming from inside us as well as all around us, cannot, to the modern mind, be anything more than the whimsical fantasies of errant seekers. Even quantum physicists know that it exists, but our fear of the unknown means we all push it away.

"Human beings who see the universe as timeless and limitless know that this force is more important than gravity, because it holds together the very fabric of existence. To collectively add to and grow this power is the most glorious thing one can do. Somehow, someway, everyone who understands this is an important piece to this all. Even you."

Dwayne turned and looked at Jeremy, giving him a sly smile. Lucy looked up at him as well, her tail thumping on the ground. Jeremy was sure she was grinning.

"Which proves, beyond a shadow of a doubt, that the universe is capricious, with a sense of humor all its own."

Jeremy smiled. Uncle D turned and headed back to the house. Lucy and Jeremy followed. When they reached the porch, Lucy walked ahead and stood at the front door, blocking the entrance. Dwayne looked at Lucy.

"Ah yes; you are right, Lucy. I forgot something." He turned again to Jeremy.

"If you choose to think that it was merely chance that on this particular night, at this particular time, you had a terrible dream that drew you to the water to see a display of nature that was truly beyond words, that is your prerogative. I choose to think otherwise. And if everything you are experiencing is not part of a divinely created dance among a multitude of beings throughout the universe but merely a fantasy collectively shared by literally a gazillion humans over gazillions of years, isn't that pretty much the same thing? I mean, think of the first time you met Baz. Think hard."

With that, Lucy and Dwayne went into the house, leaving Jeremy alone with his thoughts. Once again, the memory of him on a bike the day he learned to ride came rushing back to him. Suddenly, clear as day, there was Baz, the man he had never seen in his neighborhood before, walking a dog.

As for Lucy, she was Jeremy's constant companion. Jeremy had never had a dog, and now he felt as though he had never been without one, and that they had always been together. She felt the same way, he could tell, and she always seemed to know his thoughts and what was about to happen next. So it came as no surprise when, one day as he was cooking in the kitchen, Lucy on the floor and Dwayne dozing in the living room, she sprang to her feet and began frantically dancing around his legs, tail wagging and tongue lolling, acting as the harbinger to the loud rap that came and sent her bounding for the front door. At the knock, Jeremy knew immediately who it was — Baz. There was only one other time in his life he had heard a knock like that, so it had to be Baz. As Dwayne opened the front door, a corgi came bounding in, rolling Lucy onto the floor like they were old dog friends. Baz came in after, beaming away.

"I do believ' they be fine fren's, I do," he cackled.

Dwayne looked concerned. "Is that dog for us?"

"Ah, no, no, no. She's takin' me to her new owner and demanded we stop to see ol' Lucy here first."

Jeremy raised an eyebrow, very confused.

"Oh, they've never — I mean, never met tail ta tail ta tail," Baz added. "But she asked ta drop by just the same. All these dogs that find me, they seem to know each other, they do. An' don' ye ask, don' ye ask me her name — she hasn't tol' me yet."

Jeremy was even more confused now. Dwayne smiled benignly.

"They don' ever, ever tell me their names till they're about ta meet their person."

The two dogs were rolling on the floor as if they had known each other for years. Then the corgi went for Dwayne, jumping on him and pushing him to the floor so she could better lick his face. Jeremy never realized it until that moment, but he and Dwayne were apparently dog magnets.

Baz continued. "An don' be askin', askin' away more questions. Questions — questions be worrisome, worrisome indeed. These dogs jus' find me, they do, jus' show up. I care for 'em a bit, till they tell me it's time ta meet their person, an' somewhere along the way they tell me their name and walk me ta their new home. Their forever humans somehow, someway are startled — startled they are, but never too surprised. It always seems ta be the *exact* right time for the dog ta find 'em. Thet's jus' the way it is — it is. I met hundreds over the years and it alwa' been the same. I have, I have." Baz touched his nose and his big hat flapped. It looked as though he hadn't changed clothes since Jeremy met him on the Paternoster. From his oddly intoxicating, although slightly distasteful, smell, he probably hadn't.

"Same as yer Lucy. Had her a year; long time it was. Guess ye kept bouncing out o' her line of sight, as it were. Then up she bounded, bounded she did, an' said 'Let's git going Baz. It's me, Lucy, and it do be time to shine.' Thet musta been about the time yer dad decided to give ye a push." He stopped, turned to Jeremy, giggled a bit, and gave him a wink. "And then this here" — he nodded to the corgi — "this lil one, she got me goin' and then hollered ta stop here. Wha's that?" He looked at the little dog again. "You say its Frannie? A fine name ye have. Meet Frannie, all," Baz said with a bow. Lucy gave a yip. "An' then it hit — hit me like an acorn. She jaggled my thoughts and I remembered, I did. I do believ' I gots somethin' ta give ye, boy." He dug into his pocket and pulled out a crumpled piece of paper, then handed it to Jeremy.

"Ye need ta go there; go there soon, soon, real soon. They need a cook, they do, they most certainly do. An' they need more than that. Ye see boy, you don' know, you do not know it in any sense of the woobly words, that ye got a gift ye gots ta share. It's in ye, sleeping, but it be waking up; waking up indeedy do."

Upon hearing that, the corgi stood with her front legs on Lucy's side, smiling and panting. Jeremy unwrapped the wadded paper as Lucy sprang to her feet, emitting a delighted "Aaaaarrrrooooooooooo." The corgi tumbled over and ran to Baz.

Dwayne smiled. "That note must be good news indeed, at least for Lucy."

"Off we go, we go," Baz said. "We be wastin' some value of time, we do, an' all of a sudden Miss Frannie be wanting ta go."

The corgi ran to the door, Baz opened it, and out they went.

Jeremy stood there, trying to sort out what had just happened.

"Don't even try," Dwayne smiled, answering the upspoken question. "That's Baz. Don't question it; it'll do you no good. And listen to him. He knows of what he speaks, even if you have to translate for yourself exactly what it is he's saying. He's been like that since before you were born. Your mother loved it. She was enchanted with him."

Jeremy's eyes widened considerably.

Dwayne shook his head. "Another story for another day. Just remember, lad, most of the time things are not as they appear. Just don't you worry about Baz. He comes and goes. He seems to like you; you'll no doubt see him again. And it sounds like you'd better get going."

Jeremy looked down at the piece of paper that he had yet to read. It contained one word: "Retrouvailles."

As it turned out, Retrouvailles was a tiny, mostly unheard-of restaurant tucked away in an old neighborhood, located in the basement of an even older house. Keeping in mind the little he knew about how his life worked at the present, Jeremy went to Retrouvailles without asking any more questions. It would do him no good, and yes, questions were worrisome alright.

Retrouvailles was nice and tidy, albeit the restaurant had probably seen better days. A little sign with its name sat in the front yard as well as a large staircase: the stairs to the entrance going down, the stairs to the house going up. In front of the house sat a truck, its motor running, with an elderly couple sitting in it, smiling broadly. The woman rolled down the window.

"So glad to see you," she said. Then she climbed out of the truck and hugged him as though they had known each other for years. In retrospect, he considered that maybe they had. Like so many strangers Jeremy had met lately, she looked familiar. "You're right on time," she stated. "So sorry we can't stay to help you get settled, but Mr. Baz said you wouldn't mind a bit. Here are the keys and the deed with a note explaining all you need to know about running the place." Jeremy looked down at a sticky note affixed to the deed, which was in Jeremy's name. "Enjoy!!" was all that was written on it. Before Jeremy could respond, off the couple drove, waving out the windows. Curiouser and curiouser.

Lucy was already at the door when Jeremy let them in to the restaurant. Clean and tidy the space was indeed, although a bit tired and worn. Menus sat on a little table by the door. The place wasn't very big — perhaps ten tables fit — and the amazing smells coming from the back of the place pulled him into the kitchen. The kitchen was set and looked as if it was ready to go. Three pots were simmering on the stove and a pile of freshly cut vegetables sat off to the side on what had just become Jeremy's chopping table.

From the front of the place Jeremy heard a friendly voice call out. "Are you open? It smells delicious here." His first customers. He was off to the races, with no time to perseverate or worry.

A week later, a young woman appeared looking for work, and boy did Jeremy need the help. He had been working nonstop since the day he arrived. Recipes for the items on the small menu had been left behind, lovingly set in a notebook in a drawer in the kitchen. But after the food from his first day was gone, Jeremy was on his own for cooking, shopping, prepping, cleaning up, and waiting tables. He felt as though he was about to reach the point of collapse, even though he was, strangely enough, enjoying himself. She came in just as he was ready to open, getting settled for another busy day.

"I heard you were looking for help." Jeremy gave her a quizzical look. "Yeah, see this note?" It was exactly like the one Baz had given him, the paper crumpled and containing one word: "Retrouvailles." "I was sitting at the park watching the dogs and looking at the water, and this crazy guy wearing a crazy black hat with a dog like I'd never seen before gave it to me. I had just gotten into town" — her backpack gave that away — "and, strangely enough, the man knew it. I need a job." Jeremy smiled. Baz was at work again.

At that they both heard the front door open. Jeremy quickly nodded to her and smiled hopefully. The young woman could see Jeremy was flustered and at his wit's end, so rather than trying to explain and settle things right then, she smiled back and headed to the dining room to greet customers. There would be time to talk later.

The young woman was a wonder. She stepped right in and took over the dining room. At the end of the day, Jeremy stood in the kitchen, trying to sort and clean things up.

"Thanks."

Jeremy about jumped out of skin. As he swiveled around, he let out a little shriek. You see, Jeremy had totally forgotten about the young woman, forgotten she had been running the dining room all day, and was terrified to hear someone speak. He then remembered as he saw her standing in the doorway with Lucy leaning against her. He took Lucy's move to indicate that this person was indeed someone to trust. Jeremy smiled gratefully at her.

"I can't thank you enough," the young women continued, ignoring the shriek he'd made. "I wasn't sure what I was going to do after getting off the ferry and coming to town. If you don't need me to stay on, you can just pay me something for today and I will be out of your way. By the way, my name is Maeve."

Jeremy's face reacted in terror at the thought of another day working both the kitchen and the dining room. The thought gave him palpitations. Maeve smiled at his reaction.

"If you are as tired as I am, would it be okay if I made us both a cup of tea?"

Jeremy responded by dropping into a chair — so grateful he thought he was going to cry. Maeve took the move as a yes and headed to the stove. As she worked she began to talk. After a few seconds, Jeremy realized that he didn't need to say a word. This person, Maeve, needed to talk, it seemed, needed to process what was in her head, and the words began to flow in a rush of emotion mixed with wonder and curiosity, as if she was putting the pieces of some puzzle together for the first time and connecting the dots as she spoke. What a story it was Maeve told:. . .

PART **IV**: *Everyone has a star to follow at some time in their life. The challenge is having the courage to grab the tail.*

It was not quite two years ago when I started to question what I was doing in college. I was in graduate school at the University of Kings College in Halifax studying journalism when things seemed to lose meaning. Before that I had pretty much bounced around the Maritime provinces. I never had much of a family, and when my aunt, who I was living with before school, died, I inherited a bit of money. I finally decided I needed to do something, so I settled in Halifax to study, but things just didn't seem right. As a child I spent a lot of time on my own, reading books and living in my own world. I had the strangest dreams; not nightmares, but weird and wonderful dreams. I started poking around philosophy and religion books because of all that.

One afternoon in the library I found a book in the religion section I hadn't seen before: old, leather-bound, and titled with words of a language I had never seen. I reached for it and as soon as I touched it, a strange feeling raced up my arm, making me drop it. An old yellow piece of paper fell out. I reached down, picked it up, and contained in the note was the address for The Institute of Metaphysical Camaraderie in Nelson, British Columbia. When I looked down to pick up the book, it was gone. Well, that got my curiosity going, so I went home and sent an old-fashioned letter of inquiry to the place, and surprisingly enough got a letter in reply far faster than I would have expected. They were delighted to hear from me, and the contents of the envelope contained an odd-looking pamphlet, complete with hand-made drawings, which piqued my interest. The letter was signed by Agatha Godard, the director, so I decided to write her a personal note. As I was finishing the letter a few days later, the phone rang and, you guessed it, it was Agatha. She said she was delighted to hear I had received the materials in the mail, which was odd, as I had yet to communicate with her. She begged me to come out and look at the institute as soon as possible, and that I appeared to be a great fit. I said I would think on it. Two days later a package arrived with a handwritten note signed by Agatha, containing directions to the place, and it ended telling me I would receive $500 in cash for my "troubles" when I got there. I was beginning to run out of funds and had never been to Nelson, so I decided to throw caution to the wind and head out.

That afternoon I wandered over to the King's Students' Union to check the noticeboard for rides out west. It was much easier than I thought; in front of me at the board was a tangle of red hair attached to a very small person who was tacking up a large piece of paper with far more than enough tacks to do the job. She was having an animated discussion, as if with someone. No one else was there, and I quickly came to realize that there was another person — and that person was living inside of her. As I got to know her, it became apparent that she wasn't crazy; she didn't have a split personality. I truly believe there were two beings living in her one body. As I approached to get a closer look at the board, one hand was in a wrestling match with the other, trying to stop it from riddling the paper with tacks, desperately attempting to pull it away from the board.

"Enough of the tacks, I tell you, that's enough already!"

"Don't you dare tell me what to do! It's got to stay up."

The hand doing the pulling apparently won because both hands flew away from the board and the young woman tumbled over backward onto the floor.

"Making us look the fool again, you idiot."

"Oh, now you're blaming me again? Isn't that the way it goes; always my fault, can't accept any responsibility, can you?"

"I would if it was merited…"

The argument went on behind me as I got a look at the board, and sure enough, Tillie's notice — her name turned out to be Tillie I later found out — said, "Going to Nelson. I've got the car if you've got the cash to gas it up. Turn around if you're in."

I turned around, of course, and there sat Tillie on the floor, staring at the board and me.

We left that night on a three-day drive. Although it looked like two people, to this day I do sincerely believe there were three in the car. Let me be clear: the drive was relatively pleasant and safe. Tillie was a good driver and knew the roads enough to go around large cities and crazy freeways for the most part. The trip itself was very beautiful. But that's almost all we did, was drive. Nonstop. If Tillie had her way, I believe, and didn't have to stop for gas and when I made her so I could eat and pee, we would have never left the car. The only other thing we did was talk; or, more correctly, *she* talked the entire way. There was an ongoing conversation for the whole trip between the two creatures inhabiting that tiny body. It made it easy for me, in a way, because I was allowed to tune in and out as I chose. Tillie was quite fine when I chose to join the conversation, but also didn't mind if I stayed silent. It was evident the two had a great deal to talk about.

But, as I said, that's all we did. We did stop when I reminded her. I believe we would have run out of fuel before she realized we were low. As far as I could tell, she didn't sleep the entire drive, but I slept deeply at times, so she might have. There was only one time when Tillie engaged me, and that was once when she woke me up from a very deep sleep. I awoke to her gently tapping me on the shoulder. My head was against the passenger window, facing east. The moon was low in the sky. Dawn was just coming on, so there was a hint of light touching the sky. You know how it happens as the morning approaches, when there is this time when it is still dark, still night, but the sky gets this strange and beautiful glow to it? As I came out of my stupor, I opened my eyes slowly to the most beautiful scene and feeling. I had never seen anything like it before. The crescent moon hung over the prairie as I woke, and in the sheer intensity of it, I swear I left my body. I know it sounds weird, but I didn't, like, whoosh out of myself and zip around, I just disappeared from it; I was no longer constrained to just the space that makes up me. I simply became part of everything. I still had my own consciousness, but was filled with such intense joy I never wanted to return to my body. When I finally reconstituted myself, so to speak, I looked over and Tillie was looking at me, smiling kindly. The sun had completely risen, so some time had passed. She patted my shoulder again and started driving and talking.

(Maeve stopped talking. There was a long pause.

"I bet you think I'm loony."

Jeremy sat there, smiling at her, his eyes wide. Far from thinking her loony, Jeremy was thinking she might be the most amazing human he had ever encountered. He was entranced. Maeve had no idea the impact her story, and the similarities with his own story, was having on him. And he was smitten, as was Lucy; she lay on the floor at Maeve's feet, staring at her. Maeve continued …)

The drive continued as it had before. Tillie kept up an animated conversation for the rest of the drive, running the gamut of topics from gardening to metaphysics. Very late on what turned out to be the last day of the drive, I saw the turnoff to Nelson, but we just kept going. I was getting a bit nervous, and Tillie seemed to notice. She let me know that she knew of the place I was going, and they had recently moved up the road a bit, to "better quarters," so she would save me the hassle of finding another ride by driving me up there before heading back to Nelson. She said, "I'll grab a sandwich at my favorite place in the world before heading back to Halifax. That's why I came, and I just can't dillydally; I've got things to do."

I was confused and stunned to say the least. Things were just getting weirder and weirder. *(Curiouser and curiouser, Jeremy thought.)* About an hour later and after a short ride on a tiny ferry, we ended up in a tiny old town that looked as though it had its beginnings as a logging hub. Many of the original buildings still stood, and most had been refurbished. We headed down a street to the lakefront, where a freestanding cabin sat surrounded by a low black fence. It had a small plaque in front of the porch. It looked as though it was some kind of historical marker. Tillie assured me that this was the place and that "it looks much bigger on the inside." Her other voice muttered, "If you're batty."

I wandered in, not sure what else to do, and figured I had come that far, I might as well. The front door was unlocked and the place empty. There was a coating of dust everywhere as if the building had not been cleaned in years. There was nothing in there except for an old wooden office desk and chair. I stood staring at the room, completely confused. After a moment of staring, I noticed a small bump on the desk, under the dust. Sure enough, it was an envelope with my name on it, and inside was the promised $500 and a note on yellowed stationery from Agatha. Scrawled in impeccable cursive, it read:

> Dearest Maeve,
>
> I am so terribly sorry I was unable to wait for you, but pressing issues have called me away. Please do not be concerned in the least. Enclosed is the promised $500 to help you on your adventure. I do sincerely entreat you to continue your journey west. I promise you it will turn out for the best. I don't mean to be dramatic, but it is far more important than you can imagine.
>
> Warmest regards,
>
> Agatha

I stood there in silence. As I turned to leave, I saw Tillie in the car, giving me a thumbs-up. And then she drove off, leaving me confused and terrified in the little burg. I spent the night in a small rustic hotel, afraid, scared, and lonely, unsure what I would do next.

The following morning, I wandered down Main Street and grabbed a bite at a little grocery store. Sitting on the front porch, an old woman came out behind me and began to load her groceries in the back of what seemed to be an incredibly old truck with a little Australian shepherd in the cab, barking and whimpering as if wanting to help her. I got up and walked over to give her a hand myself. She looked up at me with deep gratitude. The experience of dawn on the prairie a few days earlier came rushing back, filling me with emotions I had never felt, but I knew at that moment I was going with her, wherever it was she was going. We chatted for a moment. I discovered her name was Wanda, and the dog was a dear old girl named Maggi. Also in the cab of the pickup was her husband, Chogan. Technically, I didn't get to formally meet him, because he was out wandering in the universe, so I was introduced to his ashes that were in a coffee can in the middle of the bench seat. Maggi and Wanda were heading to Vancouver Island to live with her daughter.

(Maeve stopped, shrugged her shoulders, and sighed.)

Of course they were, and by this time I wasn't surprised. And how much further west could I go? I offered to drive, and we set off, with me driving, Wanda and Chogan in the middle, and Maggi by the window.

Maggi didn't like busy roads, so we took a very slow, very windy route there, and it took I-don't-know-how-many hours. Unlike the first leg of the trip with Tillie, the four of us chatted like old friends catching up. Yes, it was four, as Wanda made sure to include Chogan.

We talked about our lives, about the truly wonderful world we live in, and sat in silence for a great deal of the beautiful drive. She slept a great deal, curled up with the coffee can, her head on my shoulder, while Maggi lovingly watched over them. As the hours passed and the amazing sights scrolled by, my mind emptied. I could feel care and love building inside of me in a way I had never experienced, which I let pass through me to my seatmates. Occasionally, fear or frustration would begin to creep in, edging into the corners. Fear of driving on this tiny, lonely road came and went, but also frustration and some anger at Wanda's family. Why in the world would they treat this poor dear woman like this, forcing her to make the trip by herself? What was truly overwhelming me was that as these feelings began to find their way into my mind, I would notice a crow by the side of the road as we passed. It would fly ahead a little ways and then be waiting for us again. At one time, when I was getting particularly agitated at dusk on a steep, windy, and slow portion of the drive, it actually sat in the bed of the truck, watching over us. The bird would stay until the feeling left me. After a time, these feelings subsided completely, and I was left in a state of grace I have never felt.

As we finally boarded the ferry to the island, Wanda, and especially Maggi, grew anxious. I couldn't get a straight answer as to where exactly we were going, if her family was waiting somewhere. Wanda would simply say something like, "Oh, we'll find them, I just don't want to be a burden." Maggi would whimper softly. And find them we did. They were waiting at the ferry dock, the whole family, standing in the parking lot watching the cars disembark. The old truck was impossible to miss, and suddenly I saw a woman, man, and three children running after us, waving their arms. I pulled off as soon as I could. My anger and frustration disappeared. They were worried sick. The family had planned to drive out the following week, rent a truck, and drive her back. Wanda didn't want to "be a bother," like she had said over and over, so she struck out early to surprise them. They were most definitely surprised — terrified, more precisely. It turned out someone in the town we left had seen her leave and began to worry. That person had given her daughter a call, alerting her she might be coming this way, and the family had been waiting at the ferry for over a day. They were wonderful people. They gave me a ride to the water here in town. I had no idea what was going to happen next, and then that crazy guy showed up and here I am.

$$- - -$$

Jeremy and Maeve stared at each other. That was Maeve's story. She had no concept of Jeremy's story and the similarities she would hear about when he shared it. There would be plenty of time, though. Baz was at work. The universe was at work. They were off to races. At that moment, life for the two of them became inextricably tied. And for Maeve and Jeremy, what a life it turned out to be!

Part V: *The universe is the big picture. There is no little picture.*

The knife moved in a precise manner, each cut mimicking the last as closely as possible, which would ensure consistency in cooking and flavor of the food. Breathing carefully and standing comfortably so as not to tire too quickly, he worked in a rhythmic fashion, smiling and getting lost in the process. It never got old, and new worlds opened each time.

You see, preparing food for a meal is an art and a science, as well as a spiritual experience if you manage it correctly. Looking at the process in the proper context, each step — the gathering of ingredients, cleaning, cutting, cooking, and presenting — takes on its own nuanced meaning. And when taken as a whole, the entire process can be seen as the fundamental essence of life, for food nourishes and sustains our bodies and minds. And when preparing food for others, it becomes a gesture of love and caring.

Singularly taken, the preparation of mushrooms is no different; it actually becomes even more important. Mushrooms network and communicate with each other, as do other plants. The community and connection that mushrooms maintain throughout their ecosystem helps plants on several levels. Indeed, some scientists maintain mushrooms communicate not only through electrical impulses and chemicals, but also a physical network called mycelium. These networks assist in diverting nutrient resources and communicate the presence of threats, such as disease and harmful insects. Keeping this in mind, it seems reasonable that handling mushrooms with love, care, and respect is essential.

So it was for Jeremy on this particular day as he stood quartering mushrooms and thinking about his life. This day it was chanterelles and hedgehogs that he'd foraged earlier with his granddaughter Chloe and his dog Lucy. This iteration of the hound was entering old age. Jeremy had lost track of how many Lucys there had been. It didn't really matter to him, as he considered them all to be the same dog — and, in some way, they probably were. You see, as one Lucy aged another one would appear in a litter or simply show up at the front door. The way a new Lucy materialized was a mystery, but appear she did, and Jeremy could only assume that the other dogs Baz delivered metamorphosed in the same way. It was startling at first, but over time he got used to it. Also, knowing he had a forever dog actually for forever was a comfort.

Jeremy and Chloe had decided to let Lucy pick the spot for their mushroom foraging and, as usual, she had picked a winner. The whole endeavor became an adventure, as was usually the case, full of sniffs and mushrooms galore. It wasn't a secret spot, mind you; Jeremy was happy to share in foraging with anyone he felt would be gentle to the land and was happy to guide them if they were in no hurry and enjoyed silence. Chloe and Lucy, though, were his favorite comrades to bring on such an adventure.

This was a big day. Family was coming to celebrate — celebrate his birthday, he'd been told. His seventy-something birthday it was; or so they had said, as he had forgotten to continue counting years ago. It didn't really matter what the occasion was, as he loved to cook, especially for his family. It brought him close to his father and uncle, and the joy he saw in others' faces when they ate his food put him in heaven. Jeremy smiled thinking about all this, and giggled a bit when he realized how much his life had in common with the mushroom, this day being an example of such. The life he had with Maeve was a manifestation of a network of their own. The name of their restaurant, Retrouvailles, roughly translates from the French to mean seeing someone dear to you after a very long time. Yes, Maeve and Jeremy were part of a network that was a central piece of the place. It had been there before he came, and Jeremy was sure it would continue after they were gone. The network had evolved, and the tendrils of connection continued to build and grow.

It was odd that people knew of the place but, as far as Jeremy and Maeve could tell, no one had ever advertised it in any way. They certainly hadn't. Maeve had done some research years ago and found very little information about Retrouvailles, financial or otherwise. She didn't even find much in the way of real estate documents, which seemed odd. One fact did stand out: every owner had paid their taxes on time.

The restaurant was not known for any specific type of cuisine, either, unless whatever-happens-to-appear-on-any-given-day counts as a style of cooking. With food that was usually fresh, usually local, and always made with love and care, the place was never at a loss for customers. There always seemed to be a steady stream of humans, though never too many, who loved the place. It appeared that their recipe for success was all they needed. The couple also had no doubt the universe played a major role in the whole affair. With those simple things in place, a thriving network of caring individuals revolved around the hub that was Retrouvailles. Lifelong friendships between patrons had been forged by people who'd met as strangers at the place, and people spread the word. Jeremy had long ago stopped being surprised about the connections. Recently, Maeve had led him out of the kitchen to meet a woman who had brought her daughters from Oaxaca to eat there. The two young women joked that they had tired of hearing the stories and wanted to come experience Retrouvailles for themselves. Apparently, they weren't disappointed; they three had stayed at Jeremy and Maeve's home for three days so they could extend their visit.

Jeremy's smile broadened. Yes, he was a part of a grand network, like a pebble tossed in a pond that creates a ring of ripples. The ripples had spread further than Maeve and Jeremy could ever comprehend. Jeremy laughed out loud as it came to him that they were both the pebble and one of the ripples in the water. Or were those simply the same thing? The laugh brought Jeremy back to his favorite network: the here and now.

Yes, there they were, the inseparable three — Jeremy, Chloe, and Lucy — in the kitchen, preparing his birthday meal in his tiny basement restaurant, Retrouvailles. Jeremy lived in the house above with his wife Maeve, her dog Dawn (also a forever dog and gift from Baz), Chloe and her parents, and Lucy.

On this special day, dinner was planned to be served in the backyard under a beautiful spring sky, which meant there was likely to be a rain shower or two, which was perfect. Jeremy hadn't left Vancouver Island since he had walked off the ship and saw Uncle

Dwayne again, which was so many years ago. Most of that time was spent in Victoria, usually in the restaurant or wandering the woods. Of course, there was more than just that. Love came, and then a child, and years later a grandchild. Life happened, with all its accompanying joys and sorrows.

Maeve and Jeremy's daughter, Emma, and her partner, Shawnda, were the parents of Chloe. They all lived in the house above the restaurant. They were a very close family. When Chloe came along, Jeremy and Maeve began taking more care of her and Shawnda and Emma took over the majority of the tasks at the restaurant. Not only was it a perfect fit for the adults, but Chloe loved to spend time with her grandparents, especially Jeremy. From the day she was born, the two had a special bond. As a toddler, the little girl would follow Jeremy around the restaurant, keeping her balance by holding onto Lucy. By the time Chloe was four years old, she and Jeremy seemed to communicate in a way no one else could figure out. Like Maeve and Jeremy, the granddad and granddaughter seemed to just know what the other was thinking. So it seemed logical for the entire family that as everyone grew a bit older their roles and responsibilities would change. It turned out to be a win-win solution for everyone involved.

What set Maeve and Jeremy's relationship apart from many others is that they had made sure to create time, whenever possible, for a rich shared inner life. They carved out times of silence and wonder and made it a part of their relationship. Given a chance to have dinner with friends, they would often make up some silly excuse to instead make the silence available. In that silence was where their life really happened, where they slowly learned the power of the universe that lies in silence, and the connection created with all things when one realizes this power exists within us all. If gravity is an unseen force we do not question, why is it so hard to accept the fact that unseen energy exists everywhere? They found, through time, that by focusing on the silence, joy took over and fear slid past. Jeremy learned to relish each day, whatever came. Chloe seemed to understand this at a very early age as well.

It was Chloe who brought Jeremy back to the kitchen, back to his birthday preparations.

"So are you really going away?"

He stared at the table and the bowls in front of him, taking a moment to get his bearings and bring himself back to the room. A bowl of thinly sliced mushrooms was keeping another bowl of beautiful fresh fiddleneck heads company. He had obviously been working while he'd gone wandering through time, which had been happening more and more often these days. It wasn't just visiting old memories, and it wasn't frightening in the slightest. "Time is but the stream I go a-fishing in," a favorite quote, came to his mind. Apparently, Jeremy had been fishing for a bit while preparing dinner. He sensed Chloe needed something, but he had been so far someplace else that he hadn't picked up on it. The two seldom spoke, they just *knew*.

She spoke again. "I was wondering if you really are leaving?"

It was the first Jeremy had heard of it, and he turned to her with a questioning, curious eyebrow. He was curious but not really surprised; Lucy and Chloe often knew things others didn't.

"Lucy wants to know."

Jeremy's eyes widened.

The conversation was abruptly cut short with the unceremonious entrance of another dog and Maeve, who had gained so much joy and grace over the years that it was almost overwhelming and disconcerting, while at the same time enchanting. The terrier dog Dawn was given to her by Baz on their wedding day. Maeve plopped down on the floor next to Chloe and Lucy, tucking her legs under her. So there they were, Chloe, two dogs, and Maeve sitting on the floor in the kitchen with Jeremy. Retrouvailles was closed today, so the prospect of a visit from the health inspector were slim. Dawn began carefully cleaning Lucy's ears while Maeve looked at Chloe and the two shared a knowing smile. They were two partners in crime. Chloe got up and stood behind Maeve and began braiding her long salt-and-pepper hair.

"You know," Maeve began, giving Chloe a wink, "everybody will be here by four, and although the party will be wonderful, it is going to be a zoo, and a walk beforehand would do all of us good. A walk down to the water."

Jeremy turned and looked over at them all, smiling and taking the four creatures into his mind. It never got old. He was so grateful for his life; he couldn't get over it. Ever.

"What?" Maeve asked.

Chloe answered for him. "He's just grinning his goofy grin again. You know the one. Watch it. Pretty soon he's going to be on the floor, crying and trying to hug us all at once."

"I love it," Maeve replied. "And so do you."

Chloe nodded and smiled. "Yup."

At the sound of the word "walk," Lucy and Dawn had jumped up excitedly and started uncontrollably wagging their tails.

"Also, if we don't go now, we won't get out — and I've got to get you two kids out." She smiled at Jeremy. What he wouldn't do to see that smile. "If I don't get you relaxed, when everybody gets here you will get anxious and disappear to play with the dogs."

Jeremy wasn't sure what was wrong with that, but he kept quiet. The dogs, and the children, for that matter, understood him. He didn't need to explain himself to them.

"And don't you try to bring up the argument that they need supervision. You're the one who needs supervision — everyone knows that."

Chloe chuckled. Maeve was right again. Nine times out of ten when things got crazy, Jeremy and Lucy were the ones in the middle of it.

Maeve stood. "You know I'm right. Now let's git."

Lucy and Dawn went nuts and headed to the dining room and then the front door, with Maeve following. Chloe slowly stood on a chair as Jeremy began untying his apron and gave him a hug.

"We will continue our conversation later," she whispered in his ear, then jumped off the chair and headed for the door. She stopped and turned to face him. "You can't hide from me, buddy." She paused, staring into his eyes. "You know it's going to be okay. It always is." And out the little girl ran, Jeremy smiling and following behind.

Maeve and Jeremy lived for their walks. It was a time to let the breeze blow through them, clean out the clutter of their minds, and breathe. They let the dogs and Chloe lead the way and, apparently, they were headed to what they called the cove: a little piece of beach down a rocky trail that was less visited by locals and tourists. Through the tree-lined streets and past old stately homes they made their way to the trail and headed down. There was a chill in the air, so wading in the water wasn't going to happen, unless someone accidentally ran in chasing a dog. It didn't particularly matter, though.

It was smart of Maeve to get them all down there. Their friends, and their accompanying children, would be arriving soon, and things would quickly get festive. Emma and Shawnda had said they would be around to help cook, so that was a relief. Jeremy loved these occasions, although he would at some time wish for some silence, and the walk would help prolong that need. Jeremy was also relieved to know that when the party began and everyone was there, including the unannounced and uninvited guests that would invariably appear, Maeve would become the ringmaster of the circus. Jeremy hoped he could play the trained seal.

There he stood, staring at the water and forgetting for a moment that he would eventually run out of words, the party would become a blur, and he would retire inside his mind and traverse other places. He let himself give in to the view, getting lost in it, listening with every part of himself to the surroundings. This was something he had learned more and more about since leaving the Paternoster. Surrounded by Maeve, Chloe, and the dogs, he relaxed enough to feel the seams of his existence starting to tear, opening new worlds. Maeve had strategically planned the walk in the hope this would happen. She watched him as he unconsciously stroked Lucy's head, his other hand reaching for Maeve's. She took it, acting like a child holding the string of a kite as Jeremy soared, swimming in the ocean of the divine. Maeve crawled inside his mind and soared with him for a bit, always keeping a small part of herself aware of Chloe, the dogs, and their surroundings. Time stopped, and suddenly Jeremy was everywhere all at once, spanning past, present, and future simultaneously. Images of his dad, uncle, the robin and the crow, and even Baz danced among the multitude of other realities, most of which he found unfamiliar.

Jeremy could sense a pressure at his side and slowly began to settle back into a singular reality: the present moment. Maeve had her arms around him and he could hear Chloe and the dogs. He focused his eyes on the present. Chloe was standing on a small rock outcropping left accessible by the receding tide. She had named the rock the "solargizer energizer" for whatever reason — no one knew why, and she never offered an explanation except, "C'mon, that's its name, for criminy's sake."

Faintly in the distance, Jeremy could hear singing; it was a raspy voice yodeling a tune he could not recognize. Jeremy's synapses didn't have time to fire fast enough to make the connection before Chloe began shouting joyously.

"Quinn, you're here! I knew you'd come soon. Baz, you brought her like you promised." That confirmed it. It was Baz again. Jeremy's spine began to tingle.

Lucy yowled with delight, even though as far as Jeremy could recall this iteration of Lucy had neither seen nor heard of Baz — but knew him she did. The same was true for Chloe. She was special, that he knew, but still, it was a bit strange.

Curiouser and curiouser.

Lucy bolted around the rocks, and Chloe leapt off her perch and disappeared on the other side. Dawn followed suit. Maeve and Jeremy headed toward the commotion. When they came within view, they saw that Chloe was up to her knees in the water, and a medium-sized, dark red doodle dog of a breed Maeve and Jeremy could not quite discern was jumping on her and licking her face. And there was Baz, still on the rocks, slowly rising to his feet, looking the same as always — his clothes hadn't changed, the hat was still on, and the stringy black hair flew out all around his head. Baz on the rocks was a sight and, from the angle they saw him, they could only really see his crooked smile and twinkling eyes shining under the hat. Throughout all the years Jeremy had encountered Baz, it was his eyes and smile that had affixed themselves in Jeremy's memory. A smile came to Jeremy as he imagined Baz and the Cheshire Cat sitting in a tree chatting as old friends. The old elf rose, grinning his grin, and offered a little wave.

"Is that really him?" asked Maeve. "My God, I'd forgotten all about Baz."

Jeremy hadn't. Baz, his dad, Dwayne and the robin were all tucked pleasantly in some corner of his brain. Maeve had only met Baz once.

"Have you seen him since the wedding?", she asked. Jeremy looked at Maeve and smiled. "Of course you haven't," she said. Maeve would have known if he had, as they knew everything of importance in each other's minds. And Jeremy, open and receptive, followed Maeve. She knew things he did not, emanated a power he didn't understand but was in awe of. And it seemed that Chloe had this power as well, although it was beginning to appear hers was immense. No, he had not seen Baz since the wedding — a lifetime ago. Even Uncle Dwayne had still been around then.

And suddenly, when his wedding came to mind, Jeremy was sent tumbling back in time for the second time that day. Maeve went with him on this journey, he could feel it.

It had been a beautiful day, as hopefully most weddings are in people's minds, but this day was stunning, with a light mist in the morning making it particularly perfect. It took place at the restaurant, outside. Paper lanterns hung over picnic tables where a delightful meal was shared, prepared by the wedding couple. Everyone was there, which meant not many people, but all those that were necessary. Dwayne had conjured an old friend to join them — one neither Maeve nor Jeremy knew, or had heard of, for that matter — Amara, to officiate.

Over the prior two years Dwayne had grown enchantingly at peace, emanating a warmth that was infectious. He spoke very little, conveying all he needed by his presence and actions. Emma, Maeve and Jeremy's first and only child and a toddler at the time of their wedding, could not get enough of him, so she happily spent most of the day attached to his leg, laughing and grinning. Emma kept chanting "D, D, D," while Dwayne carted her around on his leg. Dwayne was in heaven, so much so that he quickly volunteered to "supervise" her and the kids there, who really didn't require much supervision. Jeremy was envious. The ceremony had happened in the afternoon, and the day had mellowed with the sun as it moved down in the sky and attendees enjoyed themselves.

Emma suddenly shrieked with delight, pointing to a corner of the yard. A little terrier came happily trotting in, not minding the unfamiliar crowd. Actually, the dog behaved as though it was her backyard. Ironically, it was. Tail wagging, she went straight for Emma, who bumped her body over as she waddled toward the puppy. The puppy licked her face in greeting, then sauntered over to Maeve and lay at her feet. It was if she said, "Hey Maeve, I'm Dawn, your forever dog" — and this turned out not to be hyperbole. Everyone was enjoying the new visitor so much that they failed to realize the dog had brought along another guest. As if materializing out of the air — and perhaps the old pixie had — Baz wandered into the yard, tall and lanky, dressed as he always was with the signature hat. Beneath the hat was the infectious, enticing grin that was the essence of Baz. Emma immediately lost interest in Dawn and unsteadily careened as fast as she could toward him. She was literally shrieking with joy at the top of her lungs as he ran toward her with outstretched arms and then lifted her up on his shoulders in one scoop, not missing a step in his lope. This little interaction had a decidedly calming effect on the group of guests, with the assumption being that since Emma was familiar with him, he wasn't some nut who had wandered in through the bushes. Indeed, he was not; at least not to the knowledge of anyone present. "Emmer, my dear, dear Emmer! So nice ta finally see yer lil laff in person! My dearest sack o' potatoes! An' Maeve, I been busy but so wantin' ta see ye again!"

Jeremy gave Maeve a quick glance and wink. Dwayne closed in to reassure the guests, then Baz enveloped Jeremy, Maeve, Dwayne, and Emma all in a hug. Baz peeled Emma from his shoulders and placed her in Maeve's arms.

"Don' be aferd," Baz proclaimed as he turned to the group. "I'm a harmless ol' toot, I am, an' 'tis a pleasure ta meet ye. 'Tis so nice ta see ye again, me Maeve. I knewed when I first saw ye, ye and this here Jeremy were destined fer amazin' things together."

Maeve was still trying to make the connection, and then it dawned on her: the day on the bench by the water, the note, coming to the restaurant. She *had* met him before. Baz had set all of this world in motion.

Baz took off his hat and made a deep bow. It was a first for Jeremy, seeing him with the hat off. It made quite an impression: the mass of black hair growing only on the sides of his head, sticking out like a scared tumbleweed, and the bald pate. And, for the first time, the most interesting thing of all was exposed. One could not quite discern if it was actually a scar or something else, but the skin on the top of his head was an amalgam of colors — browns, reds, blacks, and tans — and contained what appeared to be a tattoo of a crescent moon a few inches above his left eyebrow. He straightened with a flourish, and with his hat held in front of him, he approached Amara deferentially.

"Dear one, it is me honor an' priv'lege ta be with ye again. I owe ye everythin' thet I cherish."

Amara came to Baz and wrapped her arms around him and although she only came to his waist, she held him closely and gently. "You are too kind, Baz. I am proud to have helped you with your gifts. It has, literally, been a millennia, I believe, since I saw you last."

The attendees watched in silence as this beautifully odd interaction took place. The varied guests in attendance had never seen either of the two, and to watch them was a bit discombobulating. Minutes ago Amara had married Jeremy and Maeve, with everyone thinking nothing of the woman with the wonderfully colored scarves that wrapped around her body.

Amara suddenly smiled, opened her arms, and called out. "I do believe it is time to dance."

And dance they did. The entire group — holding hands, holding the small ones in their arms, holding each other in their hearts — danced for the newly joined people. They danced for joy. The dogs joined in on their hind legs, intertwining themselves between people and rolling on the ground with anyone who cared to join. Rain began to fall. It was a splendid day. Over the course of it, Maeve and Baz became inseparable, often standing at the fringe of the group, deep in conversation as if they had known each other for years. Occasionally Baz would let out a giggle or snort at something she had said and do a little dance or click his heels. Jeremy never asked Maeve what they talked about; he'd actually never thought to, he was just delighted that the two had quickly become so close. He felt that, in some way, the three were now joined together, and that was a very good thing. Little Emma, the future mother of Chloe, spent the rest of the time between Dawn, Baz, Lucy, and Dwayne, wrapping herself around one or the other's legs, lolling on the bellies of the dogs and snuffling their fur, and generally being as sweet and as loving as you can imagine. She couldn't get enough of looking at Baz's head, so the hat remained off for a good share of the party. As for Baz, Jeremy had never seen the quirky yet lovable entity so full of joy, and that was saying a great deal. Baz lingered until most of the guests were gone instead of disappearing quickly, as it had been the other times their paths had crossed. Baz had always seemed to be heading somewhere.

After the guests had left and the cleanup was finished, Maeve, Dwayne, Jeremy, and Baz sat at a table. Little Emma was sound asleep in Dwayne's arms with her head on his shoulder

Baz turned to Dwayne. "I do, I do, I do believ' ta say, Dwayne, me fren', I have a big, a large favor ta be askin' from ye."

The group turned towards him. Baz had never asked a thing of anyone.

"A band o' pups be comin', I can feels it, an' I do not believe, I can do it on me own. I need yer help."

Dwayne smiled slightly and nodded. "Anything."

Baz beamed back. "I knew ye'd say thet. It's a big, a huge ask I be askin'. Ye see, I needs ye now. This minute. In fact of the matter, it be late. We needs ta go." His eyes twinkled as he finished with a slight smile. Maeve and Jeremy were never sure if it was the setting sun or their imaginations or what, but the little tattoo on his head seemed to slightly glow.

It was all a bit bizarre and surreal. Baz had always come and left without warning, but this was strange. Dwayne was taken aback. Jeremy sat and said nothing. Maeve smiled a slight smile and nodded. Emma started to fuss a bit and Dwayne handed her, carefully and lovingly, to Jeremy.

Dwayne was the first to speak. "So when, really?"

"Why now, my fren', now."

Slowly, ever so slowly, a smile appeared on Uncle Dwayne's face; his eyes brightened as if he was becoming aware of something momentous for the very first time. The rest happened very quickly, and without words. The group stood. Dwayne wrapped Emma, Maeve, and Jeremy in his arms for a long hug. He then gave Emma a kiss on the forehead. The two men walked slowly out of the backyard, the way Baz and Dawn had entered.

That was the last time Maeve and Jeremy had seen or heard from both of them. Until this day, when Baz appeared once again, after what seemed a lifetime, on Jeremy's birthday. He was ambling toward them over the rocks, smiling away, a little skip in his step. Maeve started to move toward him while Jeremy stood still for a moment, gathering his senses from the last break in time. It was a doozy.

Jeremy's brain began an attempt to piece everything together. There was Maeve, now hugging Baz with all her might, hugging him like a long-lost friend. Lucy was all over him, although there had been several iterations of Lucy since Baz was last there, so there was no possible way this Lucy would know of him; or was it in their DNA? And Chloe, his dear Chloe. Jeremy knew she was special and sometimes worried a bit about the fact, thinking that, if she had more than whatever it was that Maeve had, who knew what it might portend. It was impossible to deny, though, that Chloe was special, even more special than Jeremy had initially imagined. This was just another example of how special she was. There was something in her mind, in her spirit, that transcended anything he had ever known. She obviously knew Baz and knew Quinn was coming, and there they were, the dog sidled up to Baz, leaning next to him while she stroked her new forever dog. Jeremy wandered over to the group to meet his old friend and receive a smothering of puppy kisses by this new one. While he was kneeling next to Quinn, introducing himself, Chloe turned to Jeremy and leaned in, touching his forehead with hers. The connection was electric and immediately soothed some of the disassociation he was feeling. "It's okay, Jer." That was her pet name for her grandpa. Jeremy had never told her that it was his dad's pet name for him, as well. Perhaps she knew already. The words came as clear thoughts — images more than actual words — and were calming. The electric feeling grew and cycled through him.

"You didn't know Baz and I were friends, buddy? Really? Remember my strange dreams I came to you about? Baz showed up one night, singing a soft sleep song by my window. When I looked out, he just smiled and danced my fears away. When things get really scary, he just appears like that. Some others show up, as well, sometimes. Last time he visited, he told me Quinn would be coming, but we didn't know her name until she just told me."

Baz had started humming, looking down on the group fondly. He winked at Jeremy and patted Quinn on the head, who was staring at him with wonder and delight. Baz looked at Chloe. "Quinn be a gift from yer dear great-granny. She picked her out special fer ye." Then he turned back toward the water and began to dance the way only Baz could. As he danced his way into the water, he began to sing, or yodel, or whatever it was Baz did.

> *The sun, it do be shinin',*
> *The waves, they are gigglin'.*
> *My bonnie fren's are bright!*

It's time to be a-dancin',

A-dancin' in the light.

Time ta be a silly fool,

As fickle as can be.

So why not come a-dancin'

An' dance away with me?

By this time they were all dancing, dogs included — dancing away with Baz. The group ran deeper into the water, laughing and splashing. Suddenly, Baz stopped and took on a serious pose and then let out a whoop, the likes of which Jeremy had never heard.

He looked down at them all. "I do, I do believ', with all my heart, all my soul, right down to me very core, as right as rain, as true as true, we got a party to git to."

What a party it was.

When the wet, sandy group got back from their walk, family and friends were arriving. Their friends and such knew never to be surprised by Maeve and Jeremy anymore, but Baz was a bit much for them to take in at first. Even though you fell in love with him the minute you saw Baz, it was a love tempered with awe, curiosity, and confusion; for many, it was overwhelming. What perplexed folks was the way children and animals were drawn to him. His height, dress, and overall demeanor made one think it might be off-putting for the timid ones, but this was not the case. Of course, Baz was entertaining, but his sheer kindness and obvious love for every breath he took made him someone you just wanted to be around. You felt safe and comfortable, like an old blanket you drag out when you are feeling sad.

He stayed long, Baz did. He most often would just appear out of nowhere, cause something unexpected and glorious to happen, and then disappear. This time he lingered until just about everyone had left, a lot like the day he had absconded with Dwayne. When most of those staying over for the night surrendered to fatigue, Baz, Jeremy, and Maeve sat in the living room, enjoying the fire. Chloe hunkered in the shadows at the top of the stairs. They all knew she was there, but no one mentioned it, as it didn't really matter. She would have known anyway what was going on; she always did. Quinn sat at her side, watching intently. For the casual observer it would not have made any sense, as the group sat in silence, tired old friends at rest. For them, words really had no purpose, except to exchange pleasantries and convey thoughts to those who had yet learned how to listen. The spaces in the silence were what mattered, and in those spaces a great deal was being shared. Chloe listened carefully.

Something palpable happened in that silence, in the enormous space it created. The air thickened. A great discussion went on — Chloe could feel it from where she sat, although she could not completely understand it all. Apparently the dogs knew, it as well, as they were on high alert. The sheer focus of the group's consciousness sent waves of energy throughout the room and out into the universe. Time passed. The atmosphere finally began to soften, the air cleared. Chloe sat wide-eyed.

Baz let out a low whistle. "My, oh, my. That was something; indeed, 'twas."

Maeve spoke next, in a way that seemed like she was trying to make things definitive by sharing it out loud. "I think Jeremy needs to go alone. There is too much here to leave behind."

Baz spoke next, his voice soft and hoarse, slow and modulated. "I hate ta be an ol' poop, and that I am, but it be all or none. I don' believ' you two know all the power you have, and it be needed now, desperately needed. It be time ta unleash the power of your souls upon the universe. If gravity is as awesome as they say, an' sometimes I disagree abou' thet one, this power, collectively, is far bigger than thet. An' leaving all this behind makes that power grow, it do."

Silence again.

Quinn burst down the stairs suddenly, whimpering, followed closely by Chloe. The girl inserted herself on the couch between her grandparents, with Quinn plopping herself on top of everyone. Baz sat with Lucy, softly stroking the top of her head.

"Well," Chloe finally blurted out. "It's obvious: You both need to go, wherever it is you need to be."

Baz whispered. "They need ta be a dancin'. Maybe you can convince 'em. You felt what just happened, I know it, right as rain."

"That settles it, then," Chloe continued, acting as the judge. "You both gotta go. Didn't I tell you, Jer? Didn't I? I knew it. I dreamt it, I *felt* it. And don't think you need to stay for us, that we can't survive without you — no way, no way, no way, no how; it's just an excuse. It's not like you're dying, for criminy's sake. You've got work to do." Chloe's speech was on fire, and Quinn's tail was thumping in agreement.

Maeve leaned toward Jeremy, wedging Chloe and Quinn between them. They gently rocked that way for a time, savoring the moment, lingering in the wonderful feeling that was all around them, that they had created together.

Baz rose from his chair, holding Lucy like a baby, and wandered toward the fireplace before gently laying Lucy on a rug and kneeling next to her. "I do believ', I do indeedy believ', thet we is gettin' it all settled, it is, it is." He stretched his arms while kneeling, chuckled, and started talking quietly to himself as he curled up on the carpet next to Lucy, wrapping her in his arms. In a matter of seconds he was softly snoring, down for the count. The three others remained on the couch, smiling and staring at the fire. Chloe did the talking for Maeve and Jeremy, as was the norm, sorting it all out. Since no one else was with them, no one will ever know if it was spoken aloud or just shared between the silent spaces.

"This is so wonderful. In dreams we three go to places we can't describe, see things that we are afraid to share with others, unable to convey them in a way that would make sense and describe the beauty of it all. But dream, we do. And then we see the fear in the eyes of a lost puppy or a lonely soul who lives afraid all the time of someone who says they love them but treats them so horribly that they dare not say a word, and it aches, it aches so much. You two know this better than me and have cured your fears by reaching out to aching creatures with your love. You have so much to give, and if Baz says he needs you and you can do more, that is enough: you have to, you must. You know it, 'right as rain.'" She giggled as she spoke the last words, delighted with herself for mimicking Baz. "It is your time to shine — and maybe, someday, I can shine with you."

Jeremy and Maeve let Chloe guide them with her words. From the time they were little, they had been controlled by their fears, and by a providence of some kind, they had been led away from fear, resulting in them seeing, sensing, and *knowing* things few seldom do in this lifetime. Taming their fears by making them their own and making them their kin, a part of them, they had grown in strength. With all of that came a kind of power they never believed they could own — and share it they must, if they could. It was, indeed, their time to shine. Staring at the fire together, they drifted off to sleep.

When morning came, Baz, Chloe, Jeremy, Maeve, and the dogs were loading a few things into the car, telling the rest of the family they had decided to look at a piece of property Baz knew about just north of town. No one really believed them, but Maeve and Jeremy were unpredictable, and with this "long-lost friend" who was delightfully eccentric and had given Chloe the most amazing dog they had ever seen, they simply smiled and waved as they drove off, expecting to see them in a few days. Little did they know that if they were to ever see Maeve and Jeremy again, they would need to seek them out.

The old Comet wagon was stuffed with some bags, and Maeve and Jeremy sat in the front while Baz crammed into the rear seat with Lucy and Dawn. Baz quickly rolled both of the back windows down, hanging his head and arm out. "I hates these things, I do. I can't stay trapped here w'out the winders open. 'Twill drive me batty, batty indeed."

Chloe sat on the front steps, smiling as tears wound down her cheeks in a mixture of joy and sadness. She knew she would see them again, but it was all so big, so big she didn't know how to hold it all in. Jeremy leaned out the window, blowing them all a kiss. His heart ached, but at the same time it was filled with joy. A new adventure was beginning, the likes of which he had never seen. He winked at Chloe. She raised her hand in a little wave. At that moment, a robin landed on the railing next to her. It chirped. Chloe held out her open hand and the little bird hopped onto it. All was as it should be. Chloe and Jeremy's eyes locked — "Everything is going to be okay" — and off they drove.

Although their destination wasn't very far away, the drive was slow. Baz evidently hated cars more than any human Maeve and Jeremy had ever met; even the dogs couldn't console him. He had to keep his head out of the car, at least partially, for the drive. It rained some, but that didn't stop him; rather, it only brought the yodel in him out, which was interspersed with trying to lap raindrops from the air. It was very apparent he hadn't ridden in cars much, and the experience was obviously taxing on him. But talk he did, between slurping and yodeling.

"My, who be the ones ta build these things? Crazies. Wha' were they thinkin'? Nutters wha' they be, nutters. A person could die from lack o' air, e'en with the winders open… An' the poor pups, my, oh don' be scared, I gotcha, I do…" From Jeremy's vantage point in the front seat, it looked as though the dogs were enjoying themselves immensely.

Finally, there was a bit of silence. In that space, Chloe came to both Maeve and Jeremy's minds at the same time. They exchanged a quick, knowing glance. There she was, in their minds' eyes, only for the image to be interrupted by Baz talking again.

"Yea, let's talk abou' Chloe." Eyebrows were raised in the front seat.

"Ye know she knows all this, she do," he started. "She do, she do, know more than what you have taken yer lives ta know." It wasn't lost on both Jeremy and Maeve that he didn't mention himself. "An' she special. Don' lose her. Open yer doors ta her, help her fly when she needs. An' fly she will, she will, she will."

And then there was silence again. Baz soon pointed to a gravel road, and the old Comet rambled down it. It wound toward the water, finally ending at a tidy two-story house on the rocks, looking southwest. The mountains across the strait could be seen, as well as the open ocean to the right. They stopped and all climbed out of the car, with the dogs running to get their first sniffs of their new property. Baz ran around a bit, stretching, his mutterings to himself interjected with an occasional grunt or hoot.

"Thet's it, thet's it, ne'er again, ne'er again will I set my rump in one o' those things… An' there's yer new home. All nice an' tidy. You'll fine all ye need, I do believ', all the way ye like it. Dwayne loved it till he needed to move on, an' move on he did. Ye'll run into him sometime, I do suppose. An' move on ye will, too; ye'll know the time. I gots ta be gettin'. Godspeed, an' see ye on the ot'er side."

With a nod and a smile, Baz turned and wandered off through the open field, back toward the road. That was it. No long goodbyes, no explanations or detailed instructions; Baz just wandered off. The dogs followed him for a bit until Baz stopped and kissed each one on the nose. Then they turned and headed back to the house and Baz walked on until he faded out of sight — or, more accurately put, just disappeared.

Even though they were not far from their old home, it felt as though they were miles and miles away. Not surprisingly, they spent most of their days in silence. The pair made acquaintances with the neighbors, quickly becoming the people others went to when they were in distress. The calmness that emanated from the way they carried themselves made the two easy to approach. Maeve and Jeremy didn't mind a bit and quickly fell into their new routine. Initially, family came and went at a routine pace, but the duo disappeared a great deal, sometimes for days, with no one knowing quite where they went. The old Comet was always parked out front, whether they were at home or not. Since they had no phones or computers of any kind, it made it a bit difficult for people to keep track of the two. Letters seemed to do the trick, but their family was not accustomed to that archaic form of communication, so they came less and less frequently.

Chloe kept the connection fresh though, updating both households of the family of the others' activities, and this seemed to work. She visited her grandparents when she could, and life somehow had a way of adapting to her needs, so then she visited fairly regularly, sometimes for days. Time was marked by Chloe, counted in terms of her growing up. She never let her grandparents know when she was coming; rather, she just showed up, and if they were out, she stayed as she liked, sometimes missing them altogether. She gravitated toward a sitting room that was off of the kitchen and down a few steps from the dining room that looked out over the water with a deck opening out from it. There she would sit, looking at the water and gaining strength from the emptiness. While she looked forward to spending time with her grandparents, there was an upside to the times she arrived and found them gone. During the times she was alone, she felt a strange and powerful feeling growing within her. It was awesome, yet more than a bit scary. Sometimes she would lose herself for who-knows-how-long, occasionally coming back to this world to find Maeve and Jeremy by her side. Sometimes they were there, and sometimes they were nowhere to be found, although she was sure they were still there somehow. Chloe began to wonder if the two were trying to teach her something. With this strength came a building wave of empathy and love, although she sometimes worried she loved the feeling too much, and kept that in the back of her mind.

If time was measured by Chloe aging, it was after many years had passed when she drove to the house one evening, being pulled there by some strange and powerful urge that had descended upon her. Beside her in the passenger seat sat Quinn, with this iteration of the dog being number two or three; no one was sure, and the way one dog slid into another was outside of anyone's control, so the family had stopped counting, just as they had with Dawn and Lucy. As the car approached the house from the road, the house stood as if it was ablaze, with more lights on inside it than the two companions had ever seen. Quinn moved about restlessly in her seat, trying to make sense of this new occurrence. The two were worried at first, but as they climbed out of the car, they could hear dogs barking and the sound of laughter. There must be a party, of all things, they thought. And it was, of a sort.

Maeve greeted them at the front door. Lucy and Dawn bounded outside to kiss Chloe and play with Quinn. The old dog friends never tired of each other, and when a new version of one of them appeared, the others never missed a beat — it was if it was the same dog. Maeve was who-knows-how-old, the former salt-and-pepper hair having given way to a mane of white that only made her glow more with grace and love. They didn't speak as they hugged, then Maeve took Chloe by the hand as she led her to the sitting room. The sound of voices had become more distinct, and suddenly it hit Chloe: the voice, the lilt, the silliness, the rhyme, and the reverent irreverence could only come from one creature. Baz. That he was around meant only one thing: something was up. There was another voice she could not place. Before she entered the room there came a little singsong: "I do, I do believ' 'tis Chloe. She comes, she comes, she does." Baz's voice was different; it was deeper and softer, adding to it a sense of reverence.

As Chloe and Maeve walked into the dining room, there they were: Jeremy and Baz, of course, and another man she had never met but instantly knew just the same. As a child, in her dreams or when she was afraid, he had come instead of Baz at one time or another to give her comfort and encouragement. There they all sat on the couch and some chairs, overlooking the water. The unfamiliar man sat smiling at her, radiating tranquility and peace like the others. Uncle Dwayne — it was *the* Uncle Dwayne who Jeremy had spoken so fondly of and frequently about. They stared at each other for a time, smiling warmly at each other. It was if they had known each other for a thousand years. Perhaps they had; Chloe realized that anything was possible. Quinn ran to Dwayne's feet and lay down. A robin, *the robin,* was perched upon the couch. A crow was outside, sitting on the deck railing. Chloe could feel herself disassembling, coming apart and melting into everyone there. She lost her sense of self for a moment as she split into pieces and fragmented into space, then came back and reassembled herself, somehow changed forever, in seconds — or was it years? She didn't know. It didn't matter; nothing did during that time. When she came back to herself, the robin flitted across the room and perched upon Chloe's shoulder. Jeremy smiled and nodded. Chloe knew it was her great-grandmother, Jeremy's mother. Outside, the crow flapped its wings and cawed, jumping up and down. That had to be her great-grandpa, for sure. Smiling, Jeremy and Maeve looked at Chloe and the robin. Chloe had never seen the two so full of radiance and joy. She could feel it radiating off them from across the room. Jeremy spoke aloud, and Chloe could not remember the last time she had actually heard him speak.

"We are home, dear love. Finally home. For us to all be together, something I never dreamed could happen, is truly a gift. It is time for us to move along, to leave this to you to build upon. Our paths will cross many times in the years ahead, so there's no need to worry about that."

Uncle Dwayne turned to her, looking deep inside her being. "I see you and my dear sister" — he nodded toward the bird — "have already met." Were they spoken words or just thoughts? Chloe had no idea. Her concept of reality had been shattered, never again to be pieced together in the same way. She scanned all their faces, including the birds'. They smiled at her, projecting a deep sense of love and care. Chloe immediately could tell the crow was Jeremy's dad, the mischievous glint in his eyes made it impossible *not* to know. Jeremy spoke often of his dad's love affair with life, and it simply oozed from his being, even as a crow. She ran to Baz and Dwayne and gathered them both into a hug. Yes, they were really there — she was not dreaming. The two men pulled away and looked at Chloe.

Dwayne leaned in and whispered in her ear. "This is the moment I've been waiting for, to meet you at last. Your grandpa's mom was needed for greater things, so she left this world too early for us. I agreed to come raise Jeremy with his dad, for the two of us to guide Jeremy in finding the light, so you might come to shine on others."

The rest of the night the little group spent the hours in what appeared to be unremarkable silence while looking at the moon. Just before dawn, something did occur, something Chloe had never seen before and, as with much of the night, would never forget. Baz silently rose from his chair and walked through the door and onto the deck. He walked *through* the door — not opening it, but through it, — and continued walking to the edge of the lawn, toward the ocean. He kept walking, stepping off the grass and into the air, into the space over the ocean. Turning around to smile at the group, the smile that only Baz could wear, he then faced forward and strolled on, following the moon. Suddenly, the silhouette of a dog came running to his right side. Baz reached out, patted the dog on the head, and the two continued walking. Before giving in to sleep, Chloe saw the elf jump and click his heels, and as he did Baz and his newfound friend disappeared into the moon.

When Chloe awakened, having dreamt dreams she could never articulate to anyone, all the others were gone, except for Quinn curled at her side. She wandered the empty house knowing she wouldn't find them, but wandered still. Going from room to room, she found no trace that anyone had been there. For a moment she felt fear, but it was quickly overcome with a sense of wonder and awe. And then she felt a bit of silliness, which slowly turned into a silent laugh. She smiled as she came back to the sitting room and sat on the couch, Quinn by her side. As the light of morning began, turning away the dark of night, the words she and Jeremy often shared came to her, truer than ever before. "Everything is going to be okay." The words came to her in her head through the voice of Maeve and Jeremy. It wasn't as if they were speaking in unison; rather, it was as though their voices had merged into one voice. It was beautiful, yet indescribable. "New doors open with each generation. It is your time to shine in the dance." Absently, she stroked Quinn's head and began to laugh out loud. "Alright, alright, you all. I get it, I truly do. I see it now, and I know I'll be seeing you soon, in one way or another."

The robin and her companion the crow, both of whom had been silently watching over Chloe, flew from a branch outside the window and went to meet the others.

About the author

Brian Putnam lives in Bellingham, Washington, with his wife Robyn and their two dogs, Toula and Finn.

You can contact him at dancingdharma@proton.me.